Tales Told by a Kitchen Cat

By

Carol A. Lumm

Copyright ©2021 Carol A. Lumm

All rights reserved. This book or parts thereof are not to be reproduced in any form, stored in any retrieval system, or transmitted in any form by any means—electronic, mechanical, photocopy, recording, or otherwise—without prior written permission of the publisher, except as provided by the United States of America copyright law.

Contact: msclumm702@gmail.com

First Edition
ISBN: 9798790451522
Imprint: Independently published

Cover Illustration: Simon C. Burgos
Formatting/Editing: Carol A. Lumm
Photo: Carol A. Lumm

Skeezie

Preface

      The tales are told from the point of view of a mother cat named Skeezie to her three kittens. The cat family lives in a cozy wooden box filled with woolen cloth rags in a corner of an old fashioned kitchen. Each story is introduced in italics giving the reader a glimpse into the cat family's daily life and the relevancy of each story. Some of the events in the stores are based on the author's own family of five cats comprised of two adults and three kittens. The stories entertain as well as impart feline wisdom about their interaction with other cats, animals and humans.

                                      Carol A. Lumm
                                      December 2021

TABLE OF CONTENTS

Dedication to Life

Horsie and Ace   1

Sassy's Surprise   15

The Trouble With Busy Paws   35

Toby Meets Clan Musculus   46

The Squirrels Meet Their Match   64

Still on the Job   74

The Cat in the Window   81

The Court Jester   98

Treed Kittens   112

Winter Rescue   119

Benji Defends His Turf   127

Let's Go Exploring   134

About the Author   154

Dedication to Life

Lift your eyes upward,
Give your heart to God in prayer,
Thank him for the wisdom, understanding and love,
For the beautiful life and Heavens above,
That is life.

The morning sun and the evening stars above,
The birds singing in the springtime and winter,
The flowers that grow in all beauty,
The lakes that reflect the azure sky,
For peace and contentment within,
The woods and meadows,
In all its beauty a carpet of green grass to rest,
That is life.

Thank Him for a healthy body,
Two strong hands to work and pray,
Eyes to enjoy the beauty of Nature,
For happiness is to be able to pray and work,
To cultivate the earth and watch its results,
Harvesttime to be thankful and enjoyed,
That is life.

Thank God for true friends and family life
To guide you through life and sorrows,
To be ever helpful in time of need,
For little tiny feet in play,
With laughter and songs through the day,
That is life.

Of grown-up children and grandchildren
With love and respect
To pray and obey God's laws,
To have harmony in the home
You shall find peace and contentment,
That is life.

To be ever thankful for what you have,
To respect one's feelings and advice,
To be able to see the evening stars
At the close of the day,
For the moon to light your way,
For sleep and peace 'til another day,
That is life.

Live a righteous and helpful life,
To help one another in joy and sorrow,
To love what God gave you,
And bring your children up right
With God to be their guide,
And when your work on earth is complete,
To be able to travel to God's Kingdom in peace.

Carolyn Lumm
January 1967

Gusts of wind blew the snow in circles around the shed. It was a toolshed with all sorts of implements for fixing anything that needed it on a farm. The shed was deserted, in fact, it hadn't been used by humans for many years. It showed the symptoms of a decrepit building slowly dying from disrepair. Apparently the human who used the shed was rather disorganized. Unused materials were strewn about haphazardly. Cloth and wood were under the work table partially covering the box now inhabited by four creatures, an adult and three babies. Afternoon daylight shone through the dusty windowpanes of the only window in the shed. It faced east letting the warm morning rays of sunlight spread into the otherwise dark room. Looking carefully around, it was obvious the building had various inhabitants throughout the years. There were mice droppings, some of the wood sported teeth marks, pieces of dried plants, and a combination of dirt and chewed wood spread around the floor. Small animals had made a hole in the corner opposite the box for an entrance.

Although the door and window were closed, cold air seeped through in between the plank wall boards causing the current residents to shiver. They huddled to keep warm in a wooden box filled with cloth stored underneath a work bench against a back wall. Silently two yellow eyes, a dark pink nose, whiskers and pointed ears appeared in the opening. Gracefully the rest of the black and white furry body slid into the shed. The sound of soft whimpers emanated from the covered box in the corner. Without hesitation, four padded feet moved towards the meows.

"Hush, my children, I'm here," said a reassuring voice filled with affection.

"Mom, Mom, we missed you and were afraid something happened to you," whimpered all three kittens at once.

Their mother joined the kittens in the box gently nuzzling and licking each one in reassurance. She tiredly lay down on her side and let them cuddle next to her warm body. Eagerly they drank their fill of warm milk from their mother. Gradually tiny yawns hinted at the arrival of long awaited sleep.

"Mom, tell us a story," Skudgie sleepily asked as he settled next to his brother, Orangey, and sister, Missy.

"Okay, my children, but you must be very quiet," she said tenderness in her voice.

Her thoughts briefly touched upon the safety of them all as they huddled in the shed. Although it had been absent of humans for many years, there was always the threat of hungry predators seeking easy prey. She felt the urgency to find a safer home for her kittens. Maybe they could live with the barn cats at the farm on the other side of the meadow. Sighing, she protectively wrapped her arms around them washing each one with her moist tongue.

"It's bedtime so settle in and I'll tell you about Horsie and Ace."

"How did they meet?" inquired Missy stifling a yawn.

"Patience, Little One, you will hear the tale," Mom said tenderly.

All the kittens snuggled closer to their mother forming a multicolored ball of fur. In a hushed tone, she began her story.

Horsie and Ace

You may think Horsie was a horse, but that was not the case, in fact, it's the name of the kitten in the story. Ace was the name of the huge wild black stallion. Horsie was an orange and white Tuxedo cat with long soft fur and orange stripes that covered him like a hooded cloak. White fur stretched from chin to toes like white boots, gloves and a shirt and circled halfway round his neck like a scarf. He had a distinctive bright white circular spot on his nose. Horsie was a typical kitten and caused his mother much worry by continually wandering off. He was consumed with curiosity unlike his siblings who were content to stay close to their mother.

A perfect sunny, warm day in summer was Horsie's favorite kind of day for exploring. After tolerating a few last minute licks from his mother, he joyfully escaped outside. They lived on a farm in a hay-filled wooden box shelter safely tucked in a corner of the barn. On his way to the barn doors,

Horsie was careful to mind his manners and greeted all the creatures that lived there.

"Good morning, Mr. Sebastian. Hope your leg is better today," as the donkey nodded in response. "Hello, Henrietta, how are your chicks this morning? And greetings, Horace, see you later for my mouse-catching lesson!" as he strolled past the hen and old barn cat.

Today Horsie felt particularly adventurous. He had explored around the barn, the pig pen, the hen house and knew every corner by heart. Now he was ready for something new and anticipated a wonderful day. Without a second thought he headed for the corral. He had not met the black stallion who was being trained for racing according to the barnyard gossip grapevine. Putting some pep into his step, he was at the corral in no time. In the corral was the object of his investigation.

A huge, jet black stallion stood in the center of the corral. Sitting on the fence like crows were the humans from the farm. They seemed to be encircling the horse like wolves ready to attack. Horsie stayed out of sight behind one of the fence posts and watched the goings on. It seemed they were playing a game taking turns riding the stallion and falling off. He was puzzled by this game. The humans hooted and hollered every time the rider was kicked off the animal. Eventually they gave up the game and went away leaving the horse alone. As they passed by him he heard one of the humans say the stallion was too wild to be ridden. Horsie stayed hidden watching and trying to figure out why they wanted to ride him so badly. The horse paced and paced and whinnied around the corral as if he wanted to escape. Finally Horsie's inquisitiveness was too strong for him to resist.

"Hi, how are you today?" he asked politely as he casually strolled from his hiding place.

"Who's asking?" whinnied the stallion angrily. "If you can't help me escape, then I don't see any reason for us to be talking."

"My name is Horsie. Why do you want to escape? You get a nice corral, plenty of food, shelter and nothing to worry about. Seems like a good deal to me," reasoned the kitten. "I get to live with my Mom, brother and sister in the warm barn, fresh cow's milk, moist food once a day and mice Mom catches for us."

The black horse listened patiently to the kitten and slowly walked over to the fence for a better view of the little visitor. As he bent his head over the wooden fence, Horsie stepped back ready to sprint to safety if needed. Once he realized the horse wasn't a threat, he relaxed and sat on his haunches in the most respectful manner he could summon. He waited quietly for the stallion to speak. "I'm Ace," he matter of factly stated moving his head up and down. "You have a strange name for a kitten. How did you get it?"

"Mom started calling me Horsie when I was smaller because I am the biggest of us all. It was her nickname for me and it kinda stuck," he explained climbing the corral post to position himself on its top.

"Oh, I guess that makes sense. Well, I'm from the mountains where the rest of my herd is. We came down the mountain to feed and drink from the forest stream. Apparently we were seen by the humans and they decided to capture me. I did my best to evade them and protect my mares and foals. They finally cornered me with their ropes and brought me here. It seems these humans insist on putting themselves on my back, but I won't have it," Ace said emphatically.

"Wow! You really mean it! Wish there was something I could do. Hmmm, wait, I have an idea! Humans are easily fooled by animals. Why not let them put a saddle on your back, act like you're tamed, then when they aren't looking escape."

"Say, I think you have a good idea there, Horsie. I'll pretend to be tame then when they aren't looking I'll jump the fence and head for the mountains where they won't find me," Ace wholeheartedly agreed.

Bidding a goodnight to Ace, Horsie climbed off his perch and quickly headed to the barn. He was well pleased with himself as he returned to his mother and siblings. It made him happy to be able to help the stallion. His stomach growled reminding him it was close to dinnertime.

Several days passed before Horsie could revisit his friend Ace. For at least a week, dark foreboding clouds brought heavy rains that soaked the farmyard and fields. Horsie hadn't seen the humans too much either. He thought they probably were hiding in their houses keeping dry. Finally another sunny day came, Horsie impatiently headed to the corral and Ace. He hoped his new friend was still there as the humans liked to move animals from one place to another for some unknown reason. He rushed past his barn mates, shouting greetings over his shoulder as he hurried on his errand. Upon reaching his destination, he quickly scanned the corral for signs of Ace. "Oh, joy!", thought Horsie. There Ace was, standing near the humans who were on their usual roost and he had a saddle on his back! But upon looking at Ace more closely he appeared to be unhappy. Horsie kept himself out of the humans' line of sight and waited for them to leave. It was a painful wait while they made those funny sounds they call "laughing" and "cheering". Finally the two-leggeds took off the saddle and bridle from Ace and left. Horsie scaled the corral post quickly and anxiously shouted to Ace.

"Hey, Ace, what's happening? Haven't seen you in a long time. Why did you have a saddle on your back?" the kitten firing questions at Ace.

"Why, hello, Little Feller, glad to see you," Ace cheerfully greeted Horsie. "I put your suggestion into action. I have the humans convinced I have accepted them riding my back. Tonight I'm making my breakout. They leave me alone in the corral at night so I'm jumping the fence as soon as their houselights go out. I have to get back to my mares before another stallion takes them from me. I'd like to avoid a battle, you know."

"Gee, that's good and bad news. I'll miss you my friend, but I am glad you will be back with your family. But before you go, could you do something....I've always wanted to ride on a horse's back," Horsie asked hopefully.

"Sure, you can. Here, let me turn so you can jump onto my back. Just be careful with the claws, okay, Little Guy."

"Wow! Here I come!" as Horsie enthusiastically leaped onto his friend.

Ace slowly and carefully pranced around the corral with a very happy kitten sitting proudly on his back. Unknown to them, the humans became aware of the activity in the corral. They were flabbergasted to see a kitten riding bareback especially on an unbreakable wild horse which gave way to laughter. Fortunately the humans chose to leave the kitten and horse to their own devices.

"That was fun," proclaimed Horsie zealously. "Did you notice the humans were watching us?"

"Sure did, that oughta give them something to talk about for weeks! I got them really fooled, though. Since the last time I have fought that saddle on my back every inch of the way. Today I finally let them put that darn thing on me and, boy, were they really happy and proud of themselves. Humph, did they think that I would let them break my spirit to become their slave, no, siree, not me! They'll leave me in this corral for a few more days before making me join the other wimpy nags they ride. I think not!" he snorted indignantly.

"I guess you did fool them! So I'll say goodbye to you and I hope you find your family in the mountains. It's getting late and I better get to the barn. Maybe we'll see each other again. I'm glad we became friends," Horsie said sadly.

"Ya never know…we may meet again. See ya, Litle Buddy," Ace whinnied gently.

Horsie climbed down the fence post and pensively made his way to the barn. His mother noticed he seemed rather sad and asked him the problem. Horsie told her about his friend Ace and that he will miss him when he leaves. She licked him affectionately and lovingly to make him feel better. She made sure he was encircled by his siblings and her at bedtime so he would know he was safe.

The next morning he slowly walked to the corral hoping Ace had changed his mind, but the corral was empty. There was a lot of activity from the humans when they realized their prize stallion was gone. Frantically they saddled their horses and rode after Ace in a cloud of dust. Horsie hoped they would be unsuccessful. He decided to return to the corral later in the day to see if they found Ace. To occupy his time, Horsie stalked butterflies and grasshoppers, chased a mouse, played with his siblings and, of course, took a nap after lunch.

He wandered back to his lookout spot near the corral in the afternoon. There was a cloud of dust as the riders returned empty handed. Horsie beamed with gladness that Ace was safe in his mountain home. He heard the humans say that the black stallion couldn't be found and they didn't have the time to keep searching for him. With a bounce in his step, Horsie happily headed back to the barn and his family.

A cool gentle breeze floated over the three kittens lazily nestled under a lilac bush. The shade hid them from the hot sun's rays while they waited for their mother. She had gone to a grassy field surrounded by tall trees filled with fragrant flowers growing between dark green blades of grass. After what seemed forever, a white tail tipped with a black spot slowly bobbed through the high grass towards them.

"Look, there's Mom. I see her tail!" exclaimed Missy excitedly.

"Oh, good, I wonder if she brought us something to eat," added Skudgie.

"Really, all you ever think about is your stomach! You'll just have to wait and see what she has, if anything," Orangey interjected in annoyance.

Finally their Mom quickly covered the few remaining steps to their hiding place carrying something in her mouth. Without hesitation the kittens charged from the shaded shrub like three submarine torpedoes aimed at their mother. Happily they touched noses in greeting and each vied to be the first to rub against her soft fur as they returned to the lilac bush.

"Hello, My Children. Have you been behaving yourselves?" she inquired affectionately while dropping a large piece of cooked chicken breast.

"Oh, yes, Mother, we have," Skudgie said with much enthusiasm.

"That's wonderful. I brought you some of Cook's chicken. Eat, Little Ones. Since you have been such good kittens while I was gone, I'll tell you the story of Sassy."

"Oh, Mom, you're the best!" Orangey exclaimed with his mouth full of food. "I love Cook's food. I'm so glad we moved here from the shed."

"What's the story about?" inquired Missy.

While they ate, their mother settled herself next to her babies and waited for them to finish.

"Okay, everyone ready? This is a story about Sassy's special surprise just like you all got some unexpected juicy chicken today," said their mother beginning the tale.

Sassy's Surprise

In a corner of the kitchen out of everyone's path and eyesight was a well-used wooden wine box with old towels and rags spilling over the edge. Inside the box encircled by the warm cloth was a white kitten with large patches of black spread outward in varying shapes from her tail to head. She lived in a large house with many rooms. Sassy had lived there ever since her mother left her at the kitchen door. Eleven year old Lilly, the Abramson's youngest daughter, chose the stray kitten as her own not too long afterwards and chose "Sassy" for her name.

Sassy had two siblings, Harry and Cindy. Life was idyllic back then. They chased each other over the forest floor, around and over vegetation, tried to capture butterflies and bees, even learned how to catch mice. Then one perfectly sunny day in summer their fantasy world changed drastically forever. Their mother told them she had done her part in taking care of them and now it was time for them to be out on their own. The kittens panicked as they didn't know how to protect themselves from predators and didn't want to leave their mother. They all loved their mother who took good care of their needs and safety.

That day their mother instructed them to follow her despite their fearful protestations. They were led silently in single file out of the forest to a large green field of grass and flowers. It was difficult to keep up with their mother's pace in the grass, but the kittens determinedly followed her. Eventually a large structure appeared ahead of them. Their mother stopped and told Cindy to go with her while the rest were to wait for her return. It seemed to take forever until she returned much to their surprise without their sister. Perceiving their concerns, their mother said Cindy had a new home with caring humans. Instructing the remaining kittens to continue, they set out obediently behind her filled with increasing fear and anxiety. Abruptly they stopped at another large structure at the end of the grass field. Here she instructed Harry to go with her to his new human home. The last kitten, Sassy, waited, dreading her mother's return not knowing what was in store for her.

For what seemed like an eternity, her mother finally returned. In a matter of fact tone, Sassy was told she was taking her to a nice home with a little girl who loved cats. It turned out to be a huge house. Her mother brought the petrified kitten to the kitchen door and meowed loudly until a human in a white apron opened it. Suddenly and without a good-bye, the kitten's mother disappeared, leaving her alone and confused on the doorstep.

"My, my, what is this? What a cute kitten! Where did you come from? Are you one of Mazie's babies? You look just like her. Well, come in and let's get you some food." chortled the strange female human.

Surprised her mother had a name, Sassy meowed politely and allowed herself to be picked up and brought inside.

When Lilly, the farmer's daughter saw the kitten, she immediately fell in love with her. Cook agreed to let Lilly name the orphan and that was how Sassy started her new life even though she missed her brother and sister a lot.

As time passed Sassy had established daily rounds to catch mice and blackbirds to earn her keep. She would drink a dish of warm cow's milk before venturing out into the chilly mornings. As she searched for mice, her main meal for the day, she became acquainted with the neighboring humans and animals. One of her favorite cats to visit was Melly, an old orange tabby who was one of the Abramson barn cats. Melly wasn't allowed inside like Sassy who was Lilly's pet cat.

While on one of her hunts for a pesky and elusive mouse, Sassy encountered Melly cooling herself under a lilac bush, decided to join her friend and stretched out next to her. Melly was known by the other animals as "Telegraph Melly" because she always knew about the goings on in the valley.

"Hello, Melly, how are you today and is there any

interesting news?" queried Sassy as she settled herself on the cool leaves.

"Hey, Miss Sassy, and, no, there's nothing new. Oh, wait a minute, there is news," she said excitedly.

"What?! Tell me," Sassy said totally intrigued to hear some gossip.

"Well, last week I was at the Perry farm visiting with Sadie and her kittens. The babes really are so cute, too!" Melly crooned softly. "But, I'm getting away from the news. It seems that Kitty Black is back in the neighborhood," she stated in a disgusted tone.

Sassy's head suddenly jerked up from its resting place on her front paws.

"Kitty Black?! Who is that? I never heard of him!" Sassy responded.

"He's just a scalawag who's usually up to no good. He prides himself on being the greatest thing there was. Humph! He's just the worst cad ever!" answered Melly as she shifted her weight onto all-fours. "Oooo, it's tough getting old. It seems that all my joints and muscles ache at the same time! Have to go, the Johnson family should be putting out the leftovers. They sure do know how to eat! See you next time you're coming this way."

"Okay, see you soon...and take care of those old bones of yours," admonished Sassy.

After Melly left Sassy thoughtfully lowered her jaw back onto her front paws. She enjoyed Melly's company, especially when there was something worth gossiping about! As usual, curiosity reared its head in her thoughts. She wondered what made this Kitty Black so terrible. No one had ever mentioned him that she recalled. In the coolness she gradually closed her eyelids and started falling asleep. Unbidden, an image popped into her mind of Farmer Abramson pouring cow's milk in a bowl. Her stomach growled reminding her it must be lunchtime. Fully rousing herself Sassy trotted off to the barn.

Glad she had put some pep in her step, she arrived just as Farmer Abramson had finished pouring the milk. Not waiting to be polite, Sassy hurried over to the bowl at the same time Skeeter, a gray male barn cat, rounded the corner of the opened barn door. He was followed by the Persian clan - Mu the mother then Ahmed, Mahmood, and Saleh. Mu was fond of telling everyone that their breed was from a place far away over a very large and deep lake. All the farm animals affectionately referred to them as the Abramson Royals. Fortunately the bowl was large enough for everyone to get a taste of the warm milk. Her hunger satiated she headed to her favorite napping place under the hydrangea bush. Curling up in a furry ball on the cool dirt, Sassy closed her eyes contentedly and peacefully drifted off to sleep basking in the solitude of the bush.

"Well, what do we have here?" said a loud voice close to her ear.

Startled, Sassy instantly was on high alert with ears listening for the source of the voice. Her eyes quickly scanned all around her but didn't see anyone.

"What are you doing sleeping in my spot?" asked the voice.

"Who, who are you?" she asked nervously finally locating the source.

Peeking from under the bush was a jet black male cat. Sassy instinctively crouched ready to pounce or flee. She scrutinized the intruder for every detail. She noted his short haired coat was a shiny jet black with eyes of bright yellow peering at her that made her heart jump.

"Forgive me, Dear Lady, I am forgetting my manners. My name is Kitty Black," he replied nonchalantly bowing his head to her.

"Oh, I've heard about you," Sassy said in her most unfriendly tone.

"Really? Now what did you hear?" he asked with amusement.

"You're a cad and no good!" she snapped.

"I'm sure that's just gossip, but maybe you and I will become friends, no?" he said.

Kitty Black nodded to her again then turned and walked away from the shrub leaving a very confused Sassy behind. She lay on all four paws deep in thought feeling lost. Melly was right about the flamboyant tomcat. Finally she got up from the ground, stretched, left the shrub and ambled back to the house. A few weeks later Sassy abruptly bumped into Kitty Black as she rounded the corner of the family barn.

"Well, well, My Lovely, what a great surprise! You know you seem to be the adventurous type so let's go exploring. There's an old abandoned building in the woods I used to visit when a kitten. Recently I heard from Rupert, the old calico at the next farm, that it was a human's camp. There's a path to it on the other side of this field. What do you say?" he asked.

Sassy hesitated for a few minutes then agreed to join him. He seemed to be over-confident but there was something about him she liked that made her feel safe. Besides she loved to explore and learn more about where she lived and Kitty Black seemed to be trustworthy.

"That sounds like fun. Let's go!" she said enthusiastically.

As they traversed through the high grass and flowers of the hayfield behind the barn, Kitty Black began to playfully chase Sassy. Immediately Sassy reciprocated by stalking him as if he were prey. They bobbed and weaved gaily all the while keeping their direction towards the forest. Upon reaching the edge of the grass field her mysterious new acquaintance suddenly ducked under a low hanging branch. She followed filled with anticipation and curiosity. Kitty Black confidently steered them towards the barely visible path in the undergrowth.

"I never noticed this path before. How do you know about it?" she inquired.

"Oh, I've used it on and off for a long time. Some of my cousins lived at the camp for awhile before finding a human family to take them in where they became barn cats. My mom and sisters would visit them sometimes during the warmer weather. Mom was their mother's sister," he explained.

"Oh, how far away is it from here? I don't want to get lost," she asked worriedly.

"Not far, just over that hill ahead and down into the valley a little ways. Don't worry, I won't get you lost," he said reassuringly.

As they journeyed Sassy was fascinated by the beauty of the trees and ground flowers in the woods which reminded her of where she grew up. After awhile the surroundings started to look familiar. Unexpectedly a small creek appeared in front of them slowing their progress.

"Let's get a drink from the creek. The water is fresh and cool," suggested Kitty Black.

"Oh, great, I am thirsty!" exclaimed Sassy.

Both drank their fill. Kitty Black told her the building was nearby and they better get going before it got too late. Finally they reached the building. It was surrounded by tall grasses and shrubs in the middle of a tree grove. Sassy immediately knew where they were…it was her home! Excitedly she ran to the old familiar hole in the wall and entered the shed with Kitty Black close behind her.

"Oh, Kitty Black, this is where I grew up! I didn't know you knew about it! It's just as I remember! We would curl up together in that box in the corner to keep warm in winter. Oh, it's so good to be here again!"

"Really!? I don't remember you being here when we visited our aunt," he said surprised and slightly confused.

"Your aunt must have come here after Mom took us to our human homes. See that pile of rags over there in the corner? When we were here Mom put it in the sleeping box so we would be warm. We left at summertime. Your aunt must have moved it from the box. Can you smell the scent of your aunt and cousins? I can still smell Mom, Cindy and Harry in the cloth. I really do miss my family so much," she explained sadly.

"Why did your mom give you away?" he asked.

"According to her she had done her part raising us, it was time for her to live her own life. I guess she no longer wanted to be our mother," Sassy said with sadness mixed with betrayal in her voice.

"I'm sorry that happened to you. Have you seen your brother and sister?" he asked.

"No, but I think they live nearby, though. I recall it didn't take a long time for each of us to be dropped off at a farm. I just haven't had the courage to leave the farm and find them," she replied.

"Tell you what, since I move around from farm to farm a lot I can ask around if anyone heard of your brother and sister. Just be aware they may have been given human names but tell me what they look like so I don't find the wrong ones!" Kitty Black offered.

"Would you do that? That would be wonderful! I'll describe them to you as we go back to the farm. It must be almost time for Farmer Abramson to pour cow's milk and you know how delicious that is!" Sassy replied full of gratefulness for Kitty Black's suggestion.

They hurriedly wound their way back to the farm and, sure enough, Farmer Abramson was pouring cow's milk. As they approached the barn, Melly looked up and was shocked to see them together. Anger immediately welled up inside her. She headed directly for Kitty Black.

"Meroooow! Hisssss!" Melly snapped at Kitty Black. Without hesitation Kitty Black turned tail and skedaddled into the forest. "And don't you ever come back, you scoundrel!" hollered Melly in her most scary voice. "Humph! That will be the last of that no-good tomcat!" Melly declared turning to Sassy.

"Melly, why did you do that?" cried Sassy as she ran up to her. "He's my friend."

"How can that scoundrel be a friend? Just ask anyone around here!" Melly said with exasperation.

"He took me to my old home and even said he would try to find my brother and sister. He was nothing but a perfect gentlecat!" explained Sassy.

"Really? That doesn't sound like Kitty Black! Guess I've been listening to too much gossip, huh? Maybe you are right and he's okay…I hope he does keep his word about finding your family, though. But for now, my dear, let's treat ourselves to fresh cow milk."

A month had passed and still no sight of Kitty Black. Sassy was beginning to think that Melly was right about him being a scalawag. Sadness started clouding her spirit…she really wanted to find Harry and Cindy. Sassy avoided most of the farm activities except the daily cow's milk treat. She spent a lot of time under the lilac bush lost in her own thoughts until one day a jet black, yellow-eyed cat stuck its head under the branches startling her.

"Kitty Black, you're back!" she exclaimed happily.

"Of course, Fair Lady, did you think I had forgotten my promise? I have someone who wants to meet you so come out from that dark place," he said invitingly.

Slowly Sassy got up and peeked from under the branches. Her eyes popped wide open along with her mouth. Standing next to Kitty Black were Cindy and Harry. Instantly all three cats ran to each other, rubbed noses and bodies against each other in delirious happiness to finally be together again.

Unknown to the four cats there was a set of green eyes watching the reunion at the lilac bush.

"Well, I'll be….it seems I was wrong about Kitty Black. So glad Sassy has her family back. Well, live and learn, I guess," thought Melly with a satisfied smile.

It was an unusually hot summer's day. The air was extremely humid despite the heavy white clouds that slowly floated by in the sky. The heat from the sun created a thin layer of haze that hinted at rain, but the breeze pushed the clouds further away dispensing any thoughts of a reprieve from the heat. Gazing out the window over the kitchen table, Skeezie decided it would be best to keep her three kittens in a cooler place. Breakfast was finished hours ago but Cook Martha would be firing up the wood stove to prepare lunch. Martha was adept at performing multiple tasks and the food would be ready in no time. Walking silently to a wooden box filled with rags and kittens, their mother approached her babies. She knew the best way to keep them cool...in the cellar.

Images of her first foray into the darkness came flooding into her thoughts. The humans called it a half-cellar; the house sat half on dirt and the other half over the cellar. It was dug deep enough to hold the coolness radiating from the ground. There was a door with a latch that opened into the cellar opposite the fireplace. She had inspected it a long time ago when it was left open accidently. She recalled cautiously sniffing around the door frame as cool air emanated from below. Not sensing anything dangerous, she proceeded into the dark hole. Keeping alert for any danger, the cat tentatively placed a front paw on the top step and paused. Nothing happened, not a sound. Feeling more secure she continued to the bottom of the steps and stopped. Turning her head in all directions, she reassured herself that there were no predators to harm her. By the light of two windows she was able to distinguish shapes. Her cat eyes quickly adjusted to the dim light. The walls were made of flat stones laid on top of each other with dirt in between. The floor was all dirt except for a large protruding boulder in a corner.

There were wooden boxes stacked on one side on a high long shelf. Directly in front of the steps hanging high on the wall was a cabinet like the ones that held the kitchen dishes. It was filled with glass jars of what appeared to be vegetables from the garden. She had always wondered what happened to the vegetables and now she knew. To her amazement the floor was cool, damp and smooth. Upon further inspecting the cellar she realized there was only one entrance, a potential trap for any animal. The cat immediately knew she would have to communicate with the humans to allow her in the cellar on hot days. Thus began her cat-door campaign. She would sit by the cellar door and meow loudly on extremely warm days until Cook Martha finally understood she wanted the coolness of the cellar. She called in Tom, the handyman, to make a cat entrance in the cellar door for Skeezie and her kittens. He also made a bed high enough off the dirt floor so the feline family would be dry whenever ground soaked by rain water created a large puddle in the low part of the floor. Thanks to the kindness of the humans the mother cat was able to keep her kittens comfortable anytime the temperature became too high.

On this particular hot day Skeezie woke her kittens up with gentle licks and instructed them to follow her to the cellar.

"Mom, what is it? Is it time to eat?" asked Orangey stretching and yawning.

"No, Dear. I'm going to take you to the cellar to keep cool," replied their mother patiently.

"The cellar! Mom, you know I'm afraid of the dark!" whined Missy.

"Now, children, you know Cook Martha had Tom make a special door for us to use whenever it got too hot in the kitchen. Right now Martha is getting ready to make lunch for the humans and you know how uncomfortable it gets in the kitchen when she uses the wood stove," she explained in her most persuasive tone.

"Oh, good," exclaimed Skudgie, "that means we'll get some leftovers. I say let's get out of Martha's way until she's done cooking."

"Well, okay...but, Mom, would you tell us a story while we wait in the cellar?" Missy asked trying to keep fear out of her voice.

"Of course! I'll tell you the story of a cat named Missy," agreed Mom.

"That's my name! Is it about me?!" Missy asked excitedly.

"No, the story isn't about you, my Little One. Let's all go downstairs and get comfortable in the box and I'll tell you the tale of Missy's lesson."

Without hesitation the kittens jumped through the cat-door followed by their mother. They quickly found the wooden box with rags and settled themselves around their mother giving her their full attention.

The Trouble With Busy Paws

Once there were two boy black and white short-haired cats, Sylvester and Pumpkin, and one black girl cat, Missy. Sylvester and Pumpkin were big, really big, boys with extra long tails. In contrast, Missy had all-black fur with the hint of a white star on her chest but she also had short hair like her brothers. One morning Missy came running into the dining room filled with excitement. She jumped up onto the desk where her person, Mommy, was working and paced back and forth on the papers meowing in a staccato rhythm.

"Mommy, Mommy, you have to come outside! There's something trying get into the yard!" Missy meowed loudly.

"Why, Missy, what's the matter?" Mommy asked in surprise.

Unfortunately, Mommy had no idea what Missy was saying because all she heard was "neo-neo-neo, neo-neo".

"Come outside, Mommy," said Missy again trying to push her towards the door.

"Oh, you want to show me something, okay, let's go." She followed Missy out the kitchen door to the backyard. "Look, Missy, there's a squirrel on the fence! Go chase it away."

Without hesitation Missy quickly ran after the squirrel and chased it over the fence. The squirrel was halfway up the tree then turned and began to chatter loudly and flicked its fluffy tail at Mommy and Missy. Eventually he decided he had imparted a good piece of his mind and left. Mommy smiled amusedly and returned to the kitchen.

A few minutes later Missy again came running into the house. She ran up to her person and rubbed against her legs. Dissatisfied she wasn't getting the appropriate attention, Missy stretched herself on Mommy's leg with her claws extended. That worked!

"Mommy, I'm hungry," she meowed plaintively.

Her person only heard "new-new, neo" but attempted to understand her littlest kitten.

"Hungry? What would you like? How about some chicken?" Mommy inquired.

Missy had learned to understand the human sound for "chicken" and knew what she was getting in her dish. She immediately ran to her dish and waited patiently for her food. As soon as the dish was placed on the floor she quickly gobbled up the chicken. She especially enjoyed the gravy that came with the chicken. Missy bid her person a quick "thank you" and ran outside. For convenience Mommy kept the storm and inside doors propped open so Missy and the other housecats could come and go whenever they wanted. The only exception, of course, was at nighttime or bad weather.

Missy really enjoyed being outside especially on hot sunny days. She would play "attack", "chase", "hide-and-seek" and nap with Sylvester and Pumpkin. Missy was really happy when she and the boys chased each other. They would race around the backyard oblivious to any obstacles that might be in their way such as Mommy's plants. Sometimes Missy had to stand her ground whenever Sylvester or Pumpkin got a little too rough and defend herself in like manner. Fortunately their disagreements were brief and quickly forgotten.

When the others were napping during the day she would get bored and look for things to do. She tried catching butterflies and insects but lost interest when they wouldn't cooperate. Bees, on the other hand, were something that could keep a bored kitten enthralled. She didn't know what they were but was intrigued with the buzzing sound they made and their ability to fly in different directions instantaneously.

Missy spied a bee floating over the flowers and excitedly ran inside to tell Mommy to come look at the strange creature.

"Mommy, Mommy, there's something strange flying outside, come look!" she neo-ed to her person as she rushed inside the house.

"What is it now, Little One? You are so annoying sometimes!" as her person pretended to be exasperated. "Okay, let's go outside and see what's got you so excited."

When they went out there was a yellow and black bee hovering over each blossom of the crab apple tree next to the porch. Missy jumped onto the railing and carefully tight-roped to the mysterious insect.

"Look, Mommy, there it is. What is it?" she meowed with the hint of a question in her voice.

"Well, Little Missy, look what you've found! It's called a bee. It collects honey from the flowers, but they don't like to be disturbed. They will let you know when they're annoyed if you bother them too much by stinging you. It really hurts. I suggest you leave it alone," explained Mommy to her kitten.

Missy didn't exactly understand her person but got the idea she was telling her to be careful of that insect. The next day she saw the strange flyer again and wanted a closer look. It was again bobbing back and forth on the crab apple tree blossoms so she silently hopped onto the porch railing and slowly stalked the creature. The way it flew in different directions aroused her playful side. She tried to catch it but was unsuccessful. Determined, she continued swinging at it with her front paws but missed several times. Finally the insect left the tree and flew to the yellow flowers next to the fence. Missy jumped down and raced after her quarry. It flew close to the ground several times and Missy tried to grab it by jumping on it but failed. Suddenly her teeth closed around the prey instinctively clamping shut. Without warning Missy felt the most sharp pain ever in her mouth. She shook her head still holding the bee in a tight clasp. Eventually not being able to tolerate the pain any longer she frantically opened her mouth and let it go. In panic Missy hysterically ran to Mommy.

"Neo-neo-neoooooo," she screamed for her person.

"I don't know what you are saying but your mouth seems to be swollen. Let me take a look. Hold still! By any chance did you bother that bee!? You did, didn't you!? Missy, what am I going to do with you?" said Mommy shaking her head in frustration. "Let's get you to the doctor right away."

She quickly put Missy in the cat carrier and drove her to the vet. The doctor confirmed the bee sting and gave Missy's person some medicine to put on the kitten's tongue and roof of her mouth. When they returned home Mommy put the kitten in her favorite napping spot. Suddenly Missy was so sleepy she couldn't keep her eyes open and fell into a deep sleep. After a few hours she awoke feeling much better and sought out her person. Finding Mommy in the backyard, Missy greeted her with a very subdued "neeee" and rubbed against her legs.

"Well, hello, Sleepy Head! Feeling better? I hope you learned your lesson not to play with bumble bees otherwise they will sting you!" she said kindly.

For the first time Missy understood what Mommy was saying and promised herself she wouldn't play with any more bees. Seeing her brothers, Missy ran off to tell them all about bees and how they can really hurt a cat's mouth!

It was winter. The snow had been falling in large flakes since night and didn't show signs of letting up until later in the day. It was quiet. Cook Martha had finished for the day and left the fire burning to burn itself out. The kittens were exhausted after their day of playing in the snow. When they were cold, they would run into the barn and play in the hay spread on the floor and horse stables. Their stomachs were warmed by the fresh cow's milk the farmer poured into an old tin dish. Now they were getting sleepy after a meal of cream and ground meat. Gladly they settled into their box in the kitchen when their mother called them for bedtime.

"Mom, I'm so tired. I didn't know snow could make me tired! It was fun playing in it but after awhile my paws got so cold," said Skudgie as he yawned.

"Yes, it is. Did you know that some animals don't play in it because they have to hunt for food?" asked their mother.

"Hunt for food!? Really, Mom! What an awful thing!" Missy exclaimed in shock.

"Yes, Little One, most creatures don't have a warm kitchen and food like you do. They have to hunt other animals and forage for plants and seeds every day to take care of their families," Mom explained.

"Well, if I were on my own I would hunt mice! They come into the barn and chew up everything. Farmer Abramson always complains about them and sets traps with cheese," added Skudgie. "They must be tasty because the barn cats are always catching them."

"Now settle down, my children, and I'll tell you a story about a mouse and kitten who overcame their differences and became friends."

"Oh, great! I'm ready, Mom!" mewed Missy.

"Us, too," echoed Orangey and Skudgie.

Toby Meets Clan Musculus

Toby's nose wiggled a little then started vibrating as the scent reached his brain. A vague sense of recognition seeped into his dream of catnip, his favorite plant. Gradually as recognition turned into absolute identification, Toby opened one eye, closed it, reopened it followed by his other eye opening simultaneously. There, he had it! He knew that scent! It was his favorite meal of the day, chicken soaked in gravy. He eagerly roused himself from his nap, made sure his paws and chin were sufficiently clean, then hurried to his dish. Toby really loved his person because he, Tom, knew all of the foods a particular feline like him would eat. Toby was an average overfed six month old kitten with fluffy white fur and orange patches from the top of his head to the tip of his tail.

Next to eating Toby totally enjoyed lying in the sun as it shone warm and gentle through the large window. Whenever the sun shone, the fuzzy rug Tom had placed near the window for his kitten would absorb heat from the sun's rays. The window was a floor to ceiling sliding door that Tom opened to let in the breezes from the second floor patio. From the safety of his second floor patio railing, Toby would observe the world's happenings below him. Many other creatures passed by his perch. Each was greeted with warm regards by Toby who had no interest in chasing or attacking them. Although he did particularly enjoy watching the busily scurrying brown mice that rustled the grass below his patio roost. He spent hours just laying on the soft rug sometimes napping, daydreaming or just contemplating whatever thoughts entered his mind.

    He counted himself fortunate to have such a wonderful home with an adoring human. After eating his snack, lazily the feline stretched his full body length in front of the window again. Soaking up the sun's warmth, he meticulously cleaned his fur. If a cat could sigh, he would have sighed with happiness. Images flowed unbidden in and out of his mind as Toby slowly drifted off into the dreamland of cat adventures.

After awhile Toby felt cold air blowing over his fur. It was enough of an annoyance to rouse himself from sleep. He opened his eyes to find himself in a winter wonderland of soft snow. Immediately he closed his eyes tight and opened them again...there still was white stuff on the ground. What happened to the warm summer day in front of the window?! Confusion set in as he shook his head to clear his mind. Which was real? The ice cold wind blew flecks of the white stuff swirling around the trees. Taking stock of his predicament Toby felt a sense of relief to find himself in a warm cave out of the inclement weather. It was formed by a huge tree trunk that had fallen on top of several thick branches. He peeked out from the opening feeling despair at the amount of white stuff that covered the ground and trees. He had no idea what it was.

"Hey, what are you doing in my cave?" came a squeaky yet powerful voice from behind him.

Toby jumped hitting his head on the cave roof and turned around searching for the source of the squeaky voice.

"Who's there? Who are you? Where are you?" he asked in rapid succession.

"I am Mortimer, Laird of the Clan Musculus, who do you think I am? And you are in my cave. You must leave at once!" Mortimer ordered.

Gradually Toby's eyes became accustomed to the dim light and he was able to see two tiny pink eyes peering at him.

"I'm Toby and I didn't know this was your cave. Come out so I can see you," he demanded trying not to sound afraid.

"You can't give me orders but since you didn't know I will show myself," responded Mortimer.

Slowly and with a great deal of confidence a dark brown, tiny lithe body emerged from the darkness at the back of the cave. Toby was surprised to see a mouse appear and stand on two legs before him with a staff in its paws. He thought this was really peculiar. He had seen mice before but never walking on two legs let alone carrying a staff.

"Why, you're a mouse! How is it you stand on two feet?!" said Toby incredulously staring at this unusual creature with shock in his voice.

"Of course, I'm a mouse, you furry nit-wit!" Mortimer said emphatically. "Now, answer my question before I run you through with my staff...who are you and where are you from?"

At this point Toby was totally confused and didn't quite know how to answer the questions from this tiny mouse with the big voice.

"My name is Toby and I don't know how I got here. I thought I was napping in the warm sun and suddenly found myself here. Maybe it was all a dream, I just don't know...," he replied. "And I've never seen that white stuff outside...what is it? It's cold and wet. Where did it come from?"

"You are confused, why haven't you seen snow before? We get it every winter...you do know what winter is, don't you?" asked Mortimer.

"I don't recall any winters. This is the first time I saw this white stuff, snow, as you call it," he replied uncertainly.

"Well, anyway since you are here, I guess I should find you a place to stay. I have to forage in the snow for food and don't have time to chit-chat. Follow me and you can meet the rest of the clan. Just keep your head low so you don't cave-in the roof," instructed the mouse turning towards the tunnel from which he exited.

Since Toby had no other alternatives, he did as told, kept his head low and followed the strange mouse that walked and talked. Within a short distance the tunnel opened up into a large room where he could sit up without touching the ceiling. The ceiling seemed to glow giving warmth and light to the shadows that fell from several holes in the wall. Looking at them closer, Toby realized them to be tunnels leading to other parts of the cave as other mice came and went through them. Here, also, all of the mice talked and walked just like Mortimer. Along the edge on one side of the circular cave floor there was a raised platform containing seeds, grass, roots, leaves, oats and other vegetation. Mice were busily taking vegetation through the tunnels or entering by the same tunnel Toby used with more vegetation. The other side had what appeared to be tiny tables and chairs randomly placed on the floor.

"Well, this is the Clan Musculus," Mortimer said nodding to all the mice in sight. "As you can see we are very busy storing food for the winter ahead of us. It's going to be a really long, cold one this season and food will be scarce. Let me introduce you," he said pounding the floor with his staff. "Hear ye, Clan Musculus, we have a guest. Toby the Kitten. He has lost his way in the snow so we will give him shelter from the cold. Treat him with every kindness so that he will return the same," Mortimer declared.

Although Toby hardly heard a sound, all of the mice instantly stopped what they were doing and turned full attention to Mortimer. Looking at the gathered audience, Toby had never seen so many expressions of shock and fear on their faces. He knew he had to say something to put their minds at ease if he wanted to keep warm for the night.

"Don't be afraid, I won't hurt you, I am lost and don't know where to find my person Tom. If you allow me to spend the night in this warm place, I will leave as soon as the storm is done," he said persuasively and hoped their fears were assuaged.

The mice accepted his honesty and immediately gave him greetings of friendship. Mortimer, aware Toby was a kitten, felt no fear but compassion for him. He led Toby to a spot out of everyone's path and bade him to lay down to rest. Mortimer sat at the nearby table and sipped a drink from a cup.

"Well, Toby the Kitten, you have won the hearts of the Musculus clan, that is quite a feat!" exclaimed the mouse.

"I mean no one harm, but I am confused. How is it you mice walk and talk? I have always thought mice just squeaked and walked on all fours. My experience with mice is limited only to stories I have heard from older cats," Toby explained.

"Well, humans don't know that this particular clan exists and that we do walk and talk. If they did, they would want to dissect us to find out what makes us tick. But that's a story for another time. For now, rest until morning," Mortimer said as he stood up and disappeared down a tunnel.

Morning came along with the sounds of mice bustling in and out of the great hall. Toby opened his eyes just as Mortimer exited a tunnel. He was wearing a forest green coat of cloth and dressed for the snow still covering the ground outside.

"Well, come on, my boy, it's time to gather food before nightfall. No time for sleeping late," he said cheerfully.

"Where are you going?" Toby inquired.

"We have to get to the meadow before the eagle, Old Worchester, begins hunting. He has made it his duty to keep watch over the field waiting for small prey, especially us mice.

We must gather as much plants and seeds as we can," Mortimer explained and jumped down the main entrance tunnel.

Toby seeing there was no point in disagreeing also entered the tunnel right behind Mortimer. A large white light at the tunnel end guided him towards the cold. He was grateful his furry coat was thick enough to protect him from the wintery elements. Stepping outside he observed many mice on all-fours scurrying over the snow or under dried leafless shrubs. He wondered why they didn't walk on two legs as inside the cave but everyone was in such a hurry to accomplish their task there was no one to ask. He followed them as well as he could making his own path in the soft white powder. Glancing behind him, Toby was surprised to see that the mice were following behind him as he cleared a path for them. Very quickly they reached the meadow. Just as quickly the mice went to work. Just as they were finishing their labor, a sudden scary screeching sound came from above. Toby looked up and saw a bird with long wings and large claws diving from the sky towards the mice. The sight made the kitten feel chills and fear.

"Toby, Toby, you must run for cover. Quickly!" shouted Mortimer.

Instinctively Toby ran for his life. He didn't look back until he had reached a pile of leaves under a bush. Scanning the field for his friend, there was no one in sight just scattered mice tracks leading into the woods. Suddenly he heard a cry for help. The eagle was chasing Mortimer flapping its wings so much it created a breeze. Mortimer frantically tried to avoid those sharp talons bent on making him the predator's meal. Without a second thought of the possible danger, Toby leaped from his hiding place into the meadow. He ran, hopped, and jumped towards Mortimer.

"Mortimer, quickly, jump onto my back!" Toby shouted.

The frightened mouse did as he was told and leaped on Toby's back digging his tiny claws from all four feet into the kitten's fur. Old Worchester screamed angrily and intensified his efforts to capture not one, but two meals. Guided by his passenger, Toby dove into a thick bush of dark green needles. They waited a long time before venturing out from their safe place.

"Well, it looks like he gave up. Thank you, thank you, for saving my life," Mortimer said with gratitude in his voice.

"It was nothing. I was just helping a friend. We had better get back to the cave before he changes his mind," suggested Toby.

Neither one dared to speak as they cautiously bobbed in and out of the forest's protection to the safety of the warm Great Hall. When they appeared through the tunnel a great cheering sound came from the crowded hall. In their enthusiasm a banquet was prepared to celebrate their successful harvest, Mortimer's safe return and their new friend and protector, Toby. As the hour was getting late, the mice gradually bid Toby goodnight and disappeared into their homes leaving mouse and kitten forming a friendship.

"I must say goodnight, my friend. I am honored to call Toby the Kitten my friend. Anytime you need my help, just tell the mice where you live. They'll send me a message and I will be there to do what I can," promised Mortimer politely repressing a yawn.

"I also pledge my help, my good friend Mortimer. I also promise to never eat or chase a mouse, especially one that walks on two feet!" Toby replied.

"In the morning I'll show you where the nearest humans live. There's a young human named Lilly who loves kittens. I'm sure she'll make sure you have a home. Get some rest," said Mortimer as he disappeared into a tunnel.

Toby felt warmth radiate from his head to tail's end as the glow of friendship encircled him. He would keep his promise to Mortimer and guard the secret of mice who walked on two feet. Within an instant the exhausted kitten was sound asleep.

Gradually Toby began waking up, felt soothing heat being absorbed by his fur, remembered Mortimer was going to take him to a place to live, yawned and opened his eyes. He saw the yellow light from the sun shining through a large window. Toby stopped mid-yawn, thought that it couldn't be, he went to sleep inside a cave. He looked around, saw his person Tom in the kitchen, and jumped up instantly fully alert. Toby searched in each room for his mice friends, but found none. Sitting in the sun's rays, the confused kitten wasn't sure if it was a dream or if it really did happen.

"Hello, Sleepy Head, here's your breakfast," Tom said cheerfully as he put Toby's bowl in front of him. "Enjoy," Tom said patting Toby on the head.

The kitten realized he was hungry and eagerly gobbled up his breakfast. After cleaning his fur Toby settled into his bed to think. Did he dream about mice walking on two legs or was it real? He didn't know, so in typical Toby fashion pushed it out of his thoughts and decided it was a dream.

A few days later it was another warm day and Toby took advantage of it by sitting on his favorite patio railing. Absentmindedly gazing at the trees and bushes below the patio Toby spied a sudden but gentle rustling of the leaves under a bush. His attention focused on the movement. Watching silently the source of the movement revealed itself. It was a brown mouse! The mouse seemed to have stopped purposely in front of his patio, the tiny face turned upwards with pink eyes focused on him. It rose up from all-four feet and stood on two legs, walked a few steps into the light, and seemed to be wearing a green coat and holding a staff. The strange creature bent forward in a bow, gazed at Toby for a moment, then disappeared into the bushes again.

Toby blinked his eyes several time not sure he had really seen a mouse walk on two legs. It seemed the mouse honored him by bowing as if Toby were someone important. The little kitten felt very confused.

"Toby, come inside, it's time for dinner," Tom said placing a dish full of cooked catfish on the floor.

Without hesitation Toby almost flew into the kitchen on imaginary wings. He loved catfish. In fact, he would rather eat fish than eat a mouse!

Spring had finally arrived with the promise of warmer weather and new adventures. Gradually melting the snow and ice, the sun warmed both the earth and the kittens sitting on top of the chopped wood next to the kitchen door. They had survived the cold, windy winter staying warm with their mother in her Person's kitchen. As the days warmed, they were allowed to go outside and explore what winter had left behind. Instantly their sharp eyes detected a movement in the maple tree near the house. They didn't know what it was but it definitely deserved some inspection. It seemed to have no difficulty climbing up, down, around, or even sideways on the tree. It even seemed to float from branch to branch to tree. The creature's movement was non-stop. Whenever it stopped, the long very fluffy tail flicked back and forth when it sat on its hind legs. There was something in its mouth the creature was guarding vigilantly. Wanting to know more, the kittens ran over the remaining snow to the tree. They tried climbing the tree but their young claws couldn't dig deep into the bark resulting in them sliding back down to the ground. To make matters worse, the furry animal made a chattering sound as if scolding them for distracting it from whatever it was doing. Since they weren't making any progress in solving the question at hand, they returned to the tree stump as their mother appeared from around the house corner.

"Mom, guess what we saw? A small creature with grey fur and a long curly tail," exclaimed Missy.

"Yeah, and it seemed to float on the air as it flew from branch to branch and tree to tree," added Skudgie.

"And it spoke very rudely to us. We just wanted to get a closer look and maybe make friends," piped in Orangey.

Their mother smiled amusedly at her kittens as she nudged them towards the kitchen door. It was time for their naps and a good story would most assuredly help them fall asleep. At the door, she gently picked up each kitten by the scruff of their neck to hurry them inside. When she entered she noticed that there was no one in the kitchen except a fire in the fireplace.

"Come, children, it's time for a nap and a story," she said.

"Yippee!" as all three cheered at once.

She gently meowed as she led them into the hallway and to her favorite place. Ever since the Abramson family took her and her kittens into their home her favorite hiding place under the bottom first step of the spiral staircase. It was a floating staircase because it wasn't attached to a wall. There was a slight indentation behind the railing post and the bottom of the circular stairs. She loved the peace of her special hiding place and the country scene of the painted mural wallpaper that circled around on all four walls. The mural reminded her of the forest where she was raised with her two siblings hidden in a shed from humans and predators. Jockeying for the best position to hear a story, the kittens finally settled themselves around her like a fur shawl.

"Okay, now it's time to listen. That creature you saw in the tree is known as a squirrel. They spend most of their time hunting and storing food. Their claws are so sharp it's easy for them to jump from tree to tree without touching the ground. One of their habits is to give others a piece of their mind whenever they're disturbed in gathering their food," explained their mother, "but there are times when they just can't get their *own way. Close your eyes and listen to the tale of Harry and George."*

The Squirrels Meet Their Match

"Hey, George, did see the new neighbors?" asked Harry.

"Yeah, they sure look strange. Haven't seen anyone with such long tails on four legs before, have you?" replied Harry. "Maybe we should go say hello, George."

"Naw, we should probably wait and see what they're like," cautioned George. "We better hurry. Mabel is expecting me to bring alot of food for our cache. If I don't she'll chatter at me all night."

"Yeah, I know what you mean. Frances is the same way. Let's get going. We'll come back later and see what these new creatures are doing," agreed Harry.

Quickly the squirrels hopped from branch to branch to tree to tree in search of nuts and seeds. They stopped at their favorite birdfeeder and stuffed nuts and sunflower seeds in their mouths. Their next food source was old Mrs. Barn's backyard. She left them food on her kitchen windowsill every day. It seemed she liked watching squirrels so Harry and George made sure they acted their cutest. They particularly made sure they stopped at the Arrow store. It was easy to spot from the trees with its blue roof and many glass windows. The humans who worked there had made shelters for stray cats and left food in dishes for them. It was a delicious smorgasbord for the squirrels!

A few days later the squirrels visited their new neighbors early in the morning. They traversed from one tree to another until they reached the one next to the new neighbor's fence. They stayed near the top of the tree watching the backyard. There seemed to be a human and five creatures with long tails not as fuzzy as theirs.

"Will you look at that!" George exclaimed, "there's a birdfeeder filled with nuts just waiting for us!"

"Now, George, we should be cautious. Look over there, under the bushes, there's one of those long-tailed things. It's probably trained to kill intruders," Harry warned George.

"Well, you go ahead but be cautious. On the other hand, I'm hungry and am expected to bring something home to my wife," George responded. "Besides we were here first and any food we find is ours."

"To be on the safe side, let's just watch them for a few days so we'll know when they won't be in the yard," suggested Harry.

George thought about it for a bit then agreed. They already had a cache of nuts a few yards away they needed to store in their nest. Harry was happy George had agreed and engaged George in a game of "circle the tree" as they made their way over fences and tree branches.

After observing the human with way too many cats for several days, they finally decided to make their move into the enticing yard. Ever present on their minds was the birdseed just waiting for them. Without further discussion, George circled his way down the tree trunk followed by Harry. They tested the air for any unexpected intruders, not sensing anything unusual, they jumped onto the wooden fence. Their nails dug into the wood as they scurried towards their target.

"You know, George, this human has really made a lot of changes here. I remember when it was just grass and plants. In fact do you recall that cat that brought her babies here one summer? She used to lie in the tall grass watching her kittens play and even left them here sometimes by themselves," Harry recalled.

"Yeah, she didn't bother with us when we entered the yard to get some seeds. Wonder what happened to her and her kids," replied George.

"Who knows? I just know that it's more difficult for us to find seeds in the yard," harrumphed Harry. "Let's go down to the fence and see what there is to see," he said as he climbed down the tree trunk to the fence with George behind him.

They cautiously tight-roped on the fence their eyes scanning the terrain for any food they could pick up. Suddenly a blur of fur came charging at them from underneath shrubs startling the squirrels. To their dismay and shock three cats flew after them like torpedoes shot from a submarine. Awakening all their survival instincts they frantically scurried along the fence hoping to reach the safety of the next yard. In addition To make matters worse there was a crazed human flaying a broom at them making loud guttural sounds as if possessed. They didn't know which way to go. There was no need for conversation, they turned and ran back the way they came tripping over their own tails. The squirrels jumped onto the tree from whence they entered the yard and without a second look disappeared into the forest of leaves and branches.

"George, we have to warn the other squirrels to avoid going into that yard. They may not get out alive!" Harry said as his heart pounded so hard it almost burst.

"You'll get no argument from me. Serves us right for being so greedy. I just know I don't want to meet that demented human and the feline torpedo contingent anytime soon!" agreed George breathing heavily as they made their mad dash to safety. "How are we going to explain this to Mabel and Frances, Harry?!"

"Carefully, George, very carefully."

Sunday was a lazy day in the Abramson household after the traditional early dinner and the food and dishes were stowed in their appropriate places. Cook Martha and the other servants would gather at the kitchen table for coffee and leftover dessert. Since Cook was the only one who could read, it was her task to keep the others informed as much as possible. One particular Sunday she read a fantastic story she had found in the house library. Everyone was engrossed in the story including three kittens gathered in a furry multicolored ball underneath the butcher block table in the corner. Six wide-opened eyes focused intently on Cook as she read a story written by someone named Jules Verne. All of the human and feline listeners were totally enthralled by the story. The kittens didn't comprehend all the words but loved to listen to Cook speak. Her voice rose and fell at each exciting place. The story mentioned a machine where humans could talk and see each other between great distances without sitting next to each other. Just then their mother came into the kitchen.

"There you are, children. I thought you were napping. I know I enjoyed mine!" she smiled playfully.

"We couldn't nap, Cook was telling a story," explained Skudgie filled with excitement.

"We just had to find out what happened," Orangey added.

"Mom, Cook said something about a machine where people could talk and see each other. Isn't that a ridiculous thing!" said Missy.

"Yeah, Mom, that would never happen, right? Cook said something like 'tele...telepho' in the story, but I really didn't understand what she said," Orangey added.

"Well, what we may think is impossible today may be possible tomorrow. You know, if you all can be quiet I'll tell you the story about a cat from the future who was a true mouser and never left his post."

"Oh, Mom, would you?" asked Orangey.

"Of course, settle down now and I'll begin. Just remember it's a pretend story, okay?"

"Yay!" said all three kittens at once.

Still on the Job

Clackety-clack, chug-chug, whoo-whoo! The train announced its impending arrival into the Hudson station, its last stop. There was no raised platform as the tracks were even with the ground. Passengers had to climb up or down from the train using an inadequate small foot stool. Slowly exiting the train car, the older woman held onto the hand rails with all her strength. Seeing her uncertainty, the conductor very politely offered his assistance as she disembarked. With relief she held tight to her traveling bag and entered the station waiting room. She looked for her niece but did not see her so she made herself comfortable on one of the benches where the sun's rays brought warmth to the room.

She removed her green beret and set it on the bench next to her along with a pair of very expensive green leather gloves. She searched her bag for the small phone her niece gave her. As far as she was concerned, this effort to make her use the device was a waste of time. She loved her French table phone at home. The polished white with gold, real gold by the way, trim made her feel like a queen. This small box seemed more for someone not as cultured as she, plus it was so confusing to her. She liked the feel of placing her finger in the holes on the rotary dial and hearing the whirring sound as it rotated. She loved the clicking from the receiver as the numbers were dialed. Looking dubiously at the small telephone in her hand, she resigned herself to pecking out her niece's phone number. It rang but it was such a mechanical, cold, lifeless sound. Her niece answered and said she was on her way to the station. The lady put the annoying device away and sat quietly waiting for her niece.

Off in the distance by the cafe, she noticed something that looked like a cat. She loved cats. She had three of her own at home. She hoped her neighbor was being diligent in taking care of them while she was visiting her niece. Suddenly the cat moved. She blinked several times in confusion. Was that a real cat or not? Maybe her mind was playing tricks on her. She looked again. It moved again. The old lady had to see what it was. She picked up her gloves, hat and bag and slowly made her way towards the cat. Upon reaching the small station cafe, she examined the cat and felt reassured that it was just a statue of a crouching cat. She told the cashier that it seemed the statue was moving. With a smile and gentle laugh, the cashier said most people think the statue moves. He explained that it was modeled from the station cat that used to live there five years before. He further told her the story went that Rufus, the cat's name, was famous for being a mouser. In fact, since the cat died there hadn't been mice in the station at all. The story went that once a mouse saw Rufus ready to pounce, and being generally not very smart, they would scurry out the station and go someplace else. He surmised that although he wasn't alive now, his spirit was still chasing after mice. The old lady agreed that Rufus seemed to be on guard and as a cat person she was very pleased. Bending down, she patted the statue's head and walked back to the bench. Unheard by anyone except the cashier was a low purring radiating from the statue. The cashier smiled knowing that Rufus was always on the job.

"Merrrrow! Merrrow! Mommy! Mommy!" screamed Missy as she frantically ran to find her mother.

Instantaneously a black and white cat appeared around the corner of the barn with eyes alert to impending danger. Skeezie saw her kitten turning in circles meowing in pain trying to lick her front paw while limping. Without hesitation she ran to the young kitten's aid.

"Missy, what happened?! What's the matter with your paw?" she asked anxiously.

"The horse stepped on my paw, Mommy, and it hurts so much I can't walk on it," explained Missy plaintively.

"How did that happen and what were you doing near the horse? You know it's not safe for you kittens in the stalls. Hold still, let me take a look for any injury," she added in a calming tone.

Missy showed her mother the injured paw whining quietly and holding back tears. As there didn't seem to be a wound she licked her baby's paw gently and led her back to their bed in the kitchen.

"Mom, I'll never walk again and I definitely won't go near that horse!" said Missy emphatically as she climbed into their box, "I'm afraid I might cause more injury if I run or walk."

"Now, Kitten, you're letting your fears get the best of you. Why don't you just rest awhile and I'll tell you the story of a mysterious cat named Nala who helped a dog get over his fears," said Missy's mother as she settled herself around her daughter protectively.

The cat in the window

It was afternoon as Michael hurried home from school. His mother told him to be sure to take Spot, their collie puppy, for a walk as soon as school let out. He had said goodbye to his neighborhood school friends as they turned onto the sidewalk leading to their homes. Michael was the first one to leave the group and rounded the corner onto Maple Street. But then he saw her, Old Lady Morgan sitting on her porch sewing and looking grumpy. She never spoke to anyone and was known as the neighborhood grouch by the children. No child dared to go near her. He picked up the pace and quickly passed by her house. Walking by two more houses he turned onto the stone path to his home. His heart jumped for joy. There was his collie Spot looking out the window, tail wagging to beat a drum! Michael skipped up the steps and practically dove into the house.

"Hey, Spot, I missed you today!" he exclaimed as he hugged the dog. "Want to go outside?"

Spot wagged his tail so much his body vibrated and yipped in agreement as Michael put on the leash and led the puppy out the door into the yard. Usually Michael played with him in the yard but today he thought it would be fun to race down the block with his four-footed friend.

"Come on, Spot, I'll race you to the corner," challenged Michael.

Spot barked in agreement and both ran down the block. Michael stopped at the corner as he knew he wasn't supposed to cross the street. Spot, however, didn't know about the rule or the potential danger of crossing the street. He was so captivated by the thrill of running that he ran directly into the street. Suddenly there was a screech of terror as a riderless horse tore down the street and collided with the dog. Spot flew through the air landing hard onto the ground.

"Spot!" shouted Michael as he frantically ran to his best friend.

He found Spot lying on the ground motionless, there was blood smeared all over his white fur seeming to come from his chest. The horse was nowhere in sight having panicked and run off. Michael immediately began to cry and tried to wake up his dog, but couldn't.

"Help! Someone help!" he shouted, but no one answered his plea.

"Here, let me take a look," a voice startled him from behind.

Michael turned around and was surprised to see Mrs. Morgan wearing an old stained apron reaching for the dog. All the stories of her meanness passed in front of his mind.

"No, don't touch him, you'll hurt him, you're mean," he shouted as he protectively covered Spot with his body.

"Now, boy, you just hush and let me help your dog unless you want him to die!" she responded.

Michael didn't want Spot to die so he silently stepped aside and let Mrs. Morgan help his friend. She slowly and gently touched the animal from head to tail looking for the source of the blood. Gently turning him over a gaping wound to his shoulder and side was revealed. At the sight of the wound Michael broke into tears. Mrs. Morgan quickly took off her apron and wrapped it tightly around the dog's body covering the wound.

"Well, it could be worse, but your dog is not out of the woods yet. Let's take him to my house so I can bandage the wound better and get the vet."

Michael could only agree. He needed help and this person the children thought of as mean was willing to take care of his dog. He watched as she gently and carefully lifted up the animal and followed her onto her front porch. She set him down on a rug in front of the rocking chair and went to get some towels to keep him from going into shock. Returning a few minutes later with bandages, medicine and towels, Mrs. Morgan quickly set about cleaning up the wound.

"I sent for the vet. He'll be here shortly. Right now, I just need you to pet his head so he knows you're here," she instructed in a calm voice.

Sitting next to his best friend, Michael petted Spot's head and whispered quietly in his ear. Without warning a man's voice said hello startling Michael who jumped as Mrs. Morgan went to greet the animal doctor.

"Hello, Doc Meyers, good to see you and glad you could come right away. Michael's dog was kicked by a runaway horse and has a deep wound in his side and seems to be a little woozy, too," she explained.

"Well, I'll take a look," the vet said as he walked over to Spot and kneeled down next to him. "I assume you're Michael, lad. Let's see what the problem is, okay?"

Happy to see the vet, Michael felt more hopeful. He continued to gently pet Spot's forehead but kept his eyes focused on what the vet was doing. Finally, after examining the wounded animal the vet stood up.

"Thanks to Mrs. Morgan's quick action, your dog will be alright. He has a deep wound and a few cracked bones. He'll be out for a few more hours or so. Just keep him warm, change the bandages twice a day and give him the medication I'll give you three times a day. Now, lad, I want you to understand it was a very scary thing that happened to your dog. When he wakes up he may not be the same. He could be sad and afraid of any noise or sudden movement. He may not want to play with you or do anything else. Mrs. Morgan did a great job of fixing him up. Let him stay with her until your parents get home then have them call me and I'll explain it all to them. I'll check back tomorrow afternoon at your house. Good day, Michael, Mrs. Morgan," as he nodded to them and left.

With his mother's assistance, Spot got better and was able to move around more and more. But as the doctor predicted, Spot didn't want to play with Michael or his parents or with his dog toys. They tried everything they could think of but he just didn't seem interested in his human family. Michael was really worried. He didn't want Spot to die.

During the day Spot lay on his dog bed in front of the living room bay window in the sun. As it was getting closer to summer vacation and the weather became warmer, Michael's mother often left one of the windows open. Spot had no interest in what was happening outside. He felt fear all the time, especially at sudden noises or even the touch of Michael when he tried to hug him. He just didn't care anymore.

One particularly sunny day Spot heard a meowing sound coming from the window. He looked up and on the outside windowsill sat an orange tabby. Normally he would bark and chase it away, but now it didn't matter.

"Hey, you, down there on the floor, whatya doin'?" the cat asked startling Spot. "Want to come out and play? Bet I can beat you to the tree," the cat challenged. "My name is Nala by the way, what's yours?"

Since Spot didn't answer, she asked if the cat had caught his tongue.

"Go 'way, just leave me alone," Spot responded annoyed.

"Well, okay, for now anyways. I heard you got hurt and came to see what there was to see. I see a dog who has given up and forgotten how to be happy. I'll be back again and again until you get so annoyed you'll have no choice but to race me to the tree," Nala informed him.

And that's just what Nala did, she came to the window everyday whether it was open or not. If the window was closed she would scratch on the glass to get his attention. Gradually Spot's wound healed but his spirit didn't want to rejoin the world he once knew. He wasn't interested in eating or playing with Michael so much so it was obvious Spot was suffering from depression. Nala determined that she couldn't allow Spot to wallow in self-pity. Unknown to the depressed dog, the tabby would not give up on her mission to help him.

"Hey, Wimpy," the cat called.

"That's not my name," Spot responded with irritation in his voice, "my name's Spot. You better just remember that if you know what's good for you!"

"Well, that's an improvement! You do care about something! That's a start. Cheerio, see you tomorrow," the cat said as she jumped from the windowsill.

Spot just felt confused. He couldn't understand what was happening to him. Unable find a solution, he curled himself into a ball on the rug and took a nap. When Michael came home from school, Spot aroused himself enough to raise his head in greeting. Michael patted his head and sat down next to his friend. Talking in a calm soft voice Michael tried to be encouraging. Spot did not understand the words but he did the tone. To let his human friend know he appreciated his efforts, Spot licked his hand then lay back down and gazed off into the distance. It had been raining for a few days and there was no visit from Nala. Surprisingly Spot realized he missed the cat's visits. Finally the sun shone through the window and there sitting on the windowsill was Nala when he opened his eyes from another lengthy nap.

"Well, hello, Nala. I wondered where you had got to the past few days," exclaimed the dog.

"You do know it was raining, don't you? Did you really think I would sit on the windowsill getting wet just to watch you sleep and be all pouty?" she questioned indignantly.

"I guess not. By the way where do you live? I don't recall seeing you before," he inquired.

"Not really nearby. I do a lot of traveling. I go where my owner sends me," she replied mysteriously.

"Sounds like fun, traveling, I mean. Maybe I should just run away so I'll feel better," he pondered aloud.

"That won't do it, this is your spot, excuse the play on words, this is where you belong with Michael," Nala patiently explained. "Say, want to come outside for a bit? It's really a nice warm day and the grass is really green after the rain," she said in her most persuasive tone.

"Well, I don't know. I'm not sure I can walk that far," he hesitated.

"You won't know until you try, will you? Or are you afraid you might fall? Huh, let's see what you can do," Nala challenged.

Nala's taunts annoyed Spot enough to make him raise himself up onto all four legs. Standing in front of the window on wobbly legs, he stared at the cat and could almost see a smirk forming on her cat lips, but it was hard to discern because of all that fur.

"Alright, you orange ball of fur, you want a race to the tree, now is your chance! I'll meet you at the front door and we'll see who's faster?" challenged Spot.

Nala immediately jumped down from the sill and padded over to the front door. Spot appeared around the corner of the house. The humans usually left the back door open during the summer so it was easy for him to push the screen door open.

"Okay, Spot, you're on! At the count of three we'll race to the tree at the end of the yard. Whoever wins has to do something nice for a human," she said.

"What a strange idea, but, okay, let's go," agreed Spot.

They both went to the top porch step and assumed their best crouch position ready for take-off. At Nala's count of "three" off they went. They were nose to nose briefly but gradually Spot pulled ahead of the cat. To his surprise he was the first to get to the tree and a second later Nala arrived.

"Wow! What a rush! That was fun, let's do it again!" exclaimed Spot out of breath.

"Well, you did win but now you have to fulfill the agreement. You have to be nice to a human. That can be anyone you choose," she explained. "But for now, you might want to go inside and rest since this is the first in a long time that you've been outside."

Surprised at the suggestion, Spot decided that was a good idea since he was out of breath and did feel a little tired. Spot returned to the rug under the window, yawned and promptly fell into a peaceful sleep. He woke up at the sound of Michael slamming the front door. As always, the boy immediately greeted his four-legged friend.

"Hi, Spot, how are you doing, ol' buddy? School was boring again, glad school will be out for the summer in a few days. How was your day? Want to play in the backyard?" he asked hoping this time Spot would show some interest in playing.

To the boy's surprise Spot raised his head, licked Michael's hand, got up and walked to the backdoor wagging his tail impatiently. He was ready to go and have fun with his special person. Michael jumped up ecstatically, ran to hug the dog, opened the door and both ran joyfully outside. The next day the cat again appeared in her usual spot on the windowsill.

"Hello, ol' buddy, how ya doin'? It's good to see you up and around. Looking great, my friend!" said Nala full of nothing but encouraging words for Spot.

"It's you, how does it feel to be beaten by a dog? Not as fast as you thought, huh?!" he said jokingly.

"It feels great! Sadly I have to go. I have to be at another place tomorrow. Got things to do, you know. I've done all I can here. Good choice in being nice to Michael...he really loves you unconditionally. You two will have a long happy life together," she explained.

"What? Where are you going? I thought we were friends," he cried in shock.

"We will always be friends, but for now I am needed by a little girl who feels so alone and unloved. I must do what I can to help her. So long, my friend," said Nala as she gradually faded away into the air.

In the meantime Michael's mom noticed the cat that came to visit Spot everyday and wondered who it belonged to.

She asked her family and all the nearby neighbors including Mrs. Morgan, but no one knew anything about the feline. It became more mysterious when the cat disappeared never to be seen again shortly after Spot returned to his old happy self before the accident.

"Wow! Look at that!" a small voice exclaimed from behind a log.

The object of interest was scurrying as if its life depended upon its swift feet to reach safety. It slid under a thick bush at the end of the garden. Quickly it turned on two hind feet, its pointy nose twitching scenting the air, eyes alert, and ears listening for any unusual movement. The furry creature entered the lush foliage with its long thin tail disappearing from view.

"What a strange thing that was. It didn't look like the mice we see around here," said Missy slightly confused.

"More yet, I wonder what that thing was it was holding...it looked like a sewing needle," added Orangey.

"Very weird, right?" agreed Skudgie.

"Yeah, let's get back to the kitchen. Cook was making a cheesy dessert for the family's lunch. If we hurry we might be able to get some cheese drops," suggested Orangey idly licking his lips.

"Let's tell Mom what we saw, she might know what it was," said Missy as she turned to follow her brothers.

The three kittens ran off to the kitchen door. Cook had it slightly ajar to cool off the hot kitchen and they expertly slid through the opening. Stopping just short of the fireplace, they lined up in a neat line in front of their box. Their mother was curled up resting inside. She slowly opened her eyes, turned to look at them and smiled.

"Well, my Little Ones, what have you been up to? You look like a cat who just caught a mouse," she said in amusement.

"We were just waiting for cheese droppings from Cook's dessert. We know quite well she's not the most neat person when it comes to her fancy meals," stated Orangey.

"Mom, we saw something very strange near the garden just now. It had short white fur, a long thin tail, gray covered it from head to shoulders with a spot on its back. It ran on all fours until it reached the bushes then stood on two hind feet and disappeared. It seemed to be carrying a sewing needle in one of its paws," Skudgie breathlessly describing what he saw.

"Yeah, it wasn't like the rats or mice that live around the barn and garden," commented Missy.

A gentle amused laugh was heard from their mother.

"That was probably Hoover, the Jester. Legend says he was known as a Hood rat and a time traveler," she said.

"Who, Mom?!" asked Missy in surprise and confusion.

"Come, let's go to our special place under the stairs and I'll tell you the story of a rat who became a court jester," said Mom.

"Oh, boy, a story. But what about the cheese?" Skudgie asked with great concern.

"Don't worry about the cheese, Cook will put some in your dish for later," Mom comforted her young one.

"Wait, what is a court jester and a time traveler, Mom?" inquired Orangey.

"Be patient, you will know from the story," she explained.

Eagerly all three young felines followed their mother to their spot under the floating stairway and settled around her to hear the tale.

The Court Jester

Once upon a time a rat was born under the steps of a school where many children attended classes. His name was Hoover and was one of 13 little ratlings. Hoover had unusual markings unlike his siblings who were either all white or all gray. This particular rat had a gray hood spread down the center of his back connecting with the wide band around his waist. He was very inquisitive and wanted to explore everything around him much to his mother's dismay. She wished he would just act like a normal rat...eat, forage, and raise a family...she was disappointed in her 10th child.

On one of his forays into the nearby house Hoover was distracted by a discarded newspaper clipping about knights and castles. Immediately his imagination soared on the wings of fantasy. He wondered what it would be like to have lived in the times of knights in shining armor saving the damsel in distress. While munching on the cheese bits left on the floor in the kitchen he saw a glittery circle form next to the fireplace. It shimmered and seemed to float just above the floor. He cautiously approached the strange object, gingerly extended his paw, touching the gel-like substance and was suddenly transported back to the days of knights and kings. When Hoover opened his eyes, he shook his head to clear his thoughts, looked again and was surprised to be standing in front of a castle. The rat realized he was dressed in old raggedy clothes and standing on two legs. Instinctively his curiosity took over and he never gave his predicament a second thought. With a shrug of his shoulders, Hoover headed for the castle to see what there was to see.

      He found his way to the main square of the castle. It was filled with other rats and mice dressed similarly to him, walking on two feet, selling, fighting with swords, laughing, all the normal activities of a castle hold. He decided this was an interesting place to be and would stay for awhile. Hoover settled in and quickly adapted to his new home.

One afternoon while he was in the castle marketplace, the Court Announcer rode into the crowd, blew his long horn and began shouting.

"Hear, ye, hear, ye, a decree from the king. He is looking for a very funny jester to be hired immediately if that person could make King Larry laugh. Apply within in the castle. Drop your resume off with the Court Scribe to schedule an interview."

"Excuse me, sir, I just heard your declaration, I would like to apply but I don't have a resume. Can I apply anyway? And, by the way, what's the name of this place?" asked Hoover.

"You don't know Castle Greyhard? Where have you been, asleep for 100 years? And no, I don't know anything about the job, you'll have to see the Court Scribe," he replied and rode away in a huff.

Without hesitation the newest resident of Castle Greyhard took himself quickly to the Court Scribe. When

Hoover found the Scribe he explained his lack of a resume but assured him of his laugh-making skills. He was ushered into the presence of King Larry who just began laughing as soon as he saw the shabbily dressed rat. He especially enjoyed the idea that Hoover was a pirate pretending to be an honest citizen with his natural grey hooded head. So, he became known as Jester Hoover and for a long time he did his best to make the king laugh. To do that, Hoover had to often make himself appear very silly. As a result, Hoover promised himself that one day he would become a knight because they had a better life and did good deeds. Finally the time came for him to talk to the king about changing his position in the Court. King Larry could hardly believe his ears, a jester wanted to be a knight!

"That is the most hilarious thing I have ever heard from someone such as you, a jester! You have given me the best laugh for the day," King Larry said in between bouts of laughter.

"Indeed, I am most serious about my request," said Hoover indignantly.

"Well, it seems you are quite intent on being a knight. Before you can be knighted you first must prove yourself worthy," responded the king.

"What do I have to do?" asked the rat excitedly.

"There's a special dagger that I want. You will find it in a rock in the Bewitched Forest. You will have to avoid the vicious Mousers who guard the dagger. Your path is through the fields to the north of my castle and on into the forest," instructed the king.

"I accept the challenge. But where can I get a sword to protect myself?" he asked.

"A sword, you don't get a sword. Only knights have swords. You will have to use your wits," the king indignantly told Hoover.

"As you wish," said Hoover as he bowed slightly. "I will leave on the 'morrow for this quest."

Before leaving the castle, the rat gathered a sack of food for the journey. He made sure he got a good night's rest and arose early in the morning as soon as the sun began to rise. The castle guards opened the gate when Hoover approached them. As the castle guards closed it behind the rat they ridiculed and taunted him about his quest.

"I'll show them," Hoover said under his breath.

For days Hoover walked and walked. He ate whatever fruits and seeds he could find. Finally up ahead a bright light shone through the forest. Hoping it was the dagger, Hoover started to walk faster as he approached the stone. He remembered what King Larry said about the Tiny Mousers and carefully looked all around the boulder. He didn't see anything strange so slowly, with deliberate steps, he approached the boulder. Just as he was about to pull the dagger out of the boulder he was unexpectedly surrounded by mice dressed as warriors.

"Just what do you think you're doing, you interloper?" questioned one of the mice who appeared to be the leader.

"I'm on a quest to get this dagger for King Larry so I can become a knight," responded Hoover.

At this the mice laughed so heartedly that they fell onto the ground.

"That's really funny! King Larry wants the dagger and you want to become a knight. Now we've heard everything!" exclaimed the mouse. " I am Tristan, leader of the Tiny Mousers who guard this dagger. Only one who is worthy can pull it from the rock. If your King Larry really wanted it, why didn't he come to get it?" questioned Tristan.

"I don't know, but he promised me knighthood if I brought it back," Hoover protested.

"Let me tell you about the dagger. It was placed here by a great magician named Merlin. He told us to guard it until the right person came along who would rule the castle. He would be just, merciful and wise. Is that your good King

Larry? I think not. Maybe it's you, so go ahead and give it a try," encouraged the mouse.

"Well, I've got nothing to lose, so here goes," as he reached for the dagger effortlessly sliding it out of the boulder, "Wow, I must be the one chosen. Now what do I do?" he asked of the mouse.

"That's obvious, you go back to the castle and claim yourself a knight. Larry won't be able to do anything about it. He thinks he can just take it away from you, but he doesn't know that its powers only work for the true knight, which in this case, is you."

"Okay, I'll do just that but do you and your band want to come with me?" asked Hoover.

"Nah, I don't think so, we are just as happy to be free living in the forest, but you go ahead and see how Larry rewards you," said Tristan as he and his band faded into the forest.

Hoover arrived back at the castle feeling quite proud of himself for his successful quest. Upon showing the dagger to King Larry, Hoover was immediately put in the dungeon and the king kept the dagger for himself. The dagger had the power to defeat enemy armies in battle so King Larry went about attacking the neighboring castles. As he wielded the dagger no power emitted from it. Bewildered, the wars he started only resulted in the defeat of his armies and destruction of his kingdom. In frustration, King Larry paid a visit to Hoover who was chained to the wall in a cell with only a very small window.

"Listen, my good fellow, are you sure you got the right dagger? It doesn't seem to have any powers," complained the king.

"Oh, it does, m'lord, but only for the right one who pulls it from the giant rock. It seems you are not the one," Hoover explained.

"Well, then who is the right one? I have battles to win!" shouted King Larry.

"Why, I am, of course. How do you think I got it?" replied the rat.

"What do I have to do to get it to work?" asked the king.

"You know quite well, make me a knight as you promised because only a righteous person can hold the dagger," explained Hoover.

So Hoover was made a knight and fought many battles for King Larry. Eventually they became good friends and King Larry never again tried to underestimate the rat's ability to wield the dagger honorably. Eventually Hoover tired of knighthood and yearned for his mother and siblings and the scrapes of cheese on the kitchen floor. He turned to the Tiny Mousers for directions to the place where the circular doorway could be found. They knew right away where it was and bid him farewell and appreciation for all the good he accomplished in the kingdom. Hoover stepped through the shimmering circle and found himself back in his own kitchen and time. It was as if he had never been gone but he knew it was real for he had the dagger to prove it.

"Hey, Mom, there's a huge tree with all kinds of shiny lights and toys hanging on it!," exclaimed Skudgie excitedly.

"Skudgie, you know you aren't supposed to be in the living room," scolded his Mom patiently.

"I know, but I just had to look!" he explained.

"I love the tree, too," Missy concurred.

"Besides we were careful to stay hidden under that really big cabinet near the door so they didn't see us. Lilly's father was telling the family about a really tiny person called an Elf who wore a red fuzzy hat and sat on a shelf watching each little child to be sure they were good. If they were they would get lots of presents under the tree," said Orangey.

"The story was probably her father's favorite," Skeezie explained to her children. "Do you want to hear a story about three naughty kittens. If you can be quiet and behave yourselves long enough I'll tell it to you," she said.

"Okay, Mom, I will be on my best behavior," promised Orangey.

"So will I," agreed Skudgie.

"I will, too," added Missy.

"Okay, then, children, let's settle ourselves underneath the step where we can see the tree as I tell the tale," their mother suggested.

She led them to their floating staircase hideaway. The kittens gathered themselves into a huge furry ball with all heads towards their mother. Once they were comfortable she began her tale.

Treed Kittens

On one particular day the three boy black striped tiger kittens were at their most energetic. As soon as they saw Cook Martha putting on her coat, they knew it would be playtime soon! They all gathered in front of the kitchen fireplace politely sitting on their haunches to say goodbye. Martha admonished them to behave then left.

"Yippee!" they shouted at once and thus began the Great Chase into the forbidden living room. Rolly, the bigger kitten swished his long tail and took off at high speed. He spotted the ball that made a tingly sound under the couch, attacked it with great gusto, kicked it towards his siblings, and ran to them encouraging their participation in the game. Squeaker admired Rolly for his sense of adventure and followed right behind him. Squeaker decided to up the ante and pounced on Rolly full bodied. They rolled, kicked and bit each other, broke away and attacked each other over and over.

Fluff was the more reticent one, holding back, not ready for so much rough business, but did make the effort to join in the chases. Fluff preferred to chase Squeaker as he wasn't so mean as Rolly, so off he went after the middle sibling.

They played and chased each other for a long time, then suddenly Rolly stopped and sat still staring at the shelves with all kinds of unmoving humans perched in cages. The others stopped and followed his gaze and instinctively understood what Rolly was thinking. He studied the long straight steps with deep concentration. He saw there was a clear path from the next to bottom step to the tree with toys hanging all over it. There was only a landing place and no other walls to stop their path to the tree. Squeaker and Fluff hesitated, especially Fluff who suggested their human would be upset with them if anything was amiss. But Rolly and his ally Squeaker were not to be deterred.

"What better way to get to the tree with all those shiny things hanging on it? It would be fun to play with them, don't you think?" Rolly reasoned convincingly. "I'll go up this side of the steps and you two take the other side of the tree. Just do what I do. Bet I'll be the first to get to the top of the tree!" he challenged as he assumed his most powerful jumping stance.

He carefully measured the distance and most appropriate place to land, crouched, wiggled his body, raised his hind legs slightly and took off in flight like a bird. He landed safely on the lower shelf and waited for the others to follow. Squeaker immediately landed on the shelf on the opposite side of the tree. Fluff wasn't yet a jumper so he hung back contemplating how to best get into the tree. He decided to just simply climb up from underneath the tree. Meanwhile Squeaker and Rolly were competing for first place. In their hurry, pictures began falling from the shelves. Boom! Boom! Crash! went the pictures onto the floor. With a clearer path now visible on the shelf, Rolly reached the middle of the tree followed by Squeaker. Fluff was still on his way up the trunk when suddenly the front door opened and in came Cook Martha loaded with packages.

After awhile she realized that the kittens hadn't appeared like they usually did when she came back from the grocery store. She looked in the dining room and no kittens. Then she looked into the living room, stopped short, stood in total shock with her mouth wide open and wide-eyed. Then she spotted the addition of three kitten faces as tree decorations peeking out at her from the limbs. There they were, all three, Rolly, Squeaker, and Fluff, roosting primly in the Christmas tree, each on a branch. They had the most innocent expressions as if to say "Who, me?!"

Martha had to hide her face and turned away from them, leaned against the doorframe covering her face.

"Maybe she won't notice the mess, maybe if we look innocent and cute, she won't get angry," thought the kittens at the same time as they sat very quietly waiting.

Suddenly a loud strange noise came from their person. It started low and then gradually built in strength until she seemed about to burst. She straightened up and put both arms on her stomach holding herself as if in pain. She broke out into uncontrollable laughter as tears filled her eyes and a huge smile appeared on her lips.

"Whew!" said Rolly, "that was close. I think she's laughing so that's a good sign she's not angry with us. Just sit still, maybe she'll rescue us from this tree."

And that's what happened. She carefully untangled all three culprits making sure not to disturb any of the decorations, took them back to the kitchen and put them in their box with their mother.

Skeezie sat on the windowsill in her person Lilly's room in the early morning sunshine. The bedroom and the kitchen were the only rooms in the house she was allowed to be in. Impatiently her tail swished back and forth waiting for Lilly to open her eyes. Suddenly her tail stopped, Lilly moved under the covers then opened her eyes and looked out the window. The first to greet her in the morning was her favorite cat Skeezie.

"Good morning, Skeezie. It's a beautiful day, huh," she said. "Ow, my stomach hurts," as she placed her hand on her stomach. "Must have been something I ate. My eyes are itchy and my nose runny. It must be hot outside, I'm really sweaty. Mom! Mom! I don't feel well," she fearfully shouted.

Lilly's mother ran into her daughter's room full of concern.

"What's the matter, Darling?" she asked in a panicky voice.

"I don't feel good, my stomach hurts, my eyes are itchy and I have a runny nose," Lilly cried and clung to her mother.

"Goodness, you're hot. I'll get a cold wet cloth to put on your head. Stay in bed and stay covered up. I'll be right back," and she quickly left the room.

Her mother returned with a basin and a cold washcloth, some water in a glass and a pill. After administering to her daughter, her mother quietly left the room to let her fall asleep.

"Oh, Skeezie, I don't feel good," the child moaned.

Skeezie jumped off the windowsill and landed lightly at the foot of the bed. Carefully she walked up to Lilly, mewed softly and gently rubbed her head against her person's forehead. Then the cat lay down next to her and Lilly *protectively placed her arm around her furry friend. Skeezie faithfully guarded her sleeping person from any harm.*

A loud voice startled the cat, but when she recognized who it was, she relaxed, lowered her head back onto her front paws. The voice belonged to her person's father, Mr. Abramson. His face expressed great concern for his youngest child.

"What's the matter with my favorite girl?" he asked trying to be cheerful as he sat next to her on her bed.

"Oh, Dad, of course, I'm your favorite girl, I'm the only girl you have!" Lilly replied.

"Looks like you don't have to go to school today. Say, what about a story about when Uncle Steve and I were young? I bet Skeezie would like to hear it, too. Right, Skeezie?" acknowledging the furry ball lying curled next to his daughter.

Skeezie raised her head at the sound of her name and politely meowed in agreement.

"Dad, please tell it. I love to hear about you growing up!" said Lilly, her face lighting up and a smile playfully appearing on her lips.

"Great! Here goes," he said. "Close your eyes so you can picture it," he instructed.

Lilly closed her eyes and let the story play in her mind as if she were watching it from a distance. Skeezie nuzzled Lilly's chin then closed her eyes, ears directed towards her person's father as he began his tale. Suddenly she heard a movement under the dresser by the door. She recognized the furry faces peering out from underneath. With some annoyance, Skeezie jumped down from her post and went to her kittens.

"What are you three kittens doing here? You're supposed to be in the kitchen, my children!" admonishing her kits.

"We wondered where you were and then we heard your person Lilly scream. We hurried upstairs being sure no one saw us," explained Skudgie.

"Can we stay to listen to her father's story, Mom, please?" asked Missy.

"Wellll, you cared enough to come see what was happening so I guess you can stay but you must be very, very quiet," agreed Skeezie. "You need to stay under the dresser but I must go back to Lilly so I can comfort her. When her father leaves all three of you have to go back downstairs undetected," their mother instructed them.

The kittens agreed and quietly scooted deep under the dresser and lay next to each other with their eyes focused on Lilly's father. Skeezie returned to her place next to Lilly and settled in to also listen to the story.

Winter Rescue

In neutral colors of black, white and gray, winter can look cold. Even now I can feel the cold dampness penetrating to my bones and the wind blowing through me. I know all too well the dangers of frozen ice, below zero temperatures, no heat, strong Westerly winds and the howl of the wind at night. But then there are warm days when we welcome the sun's heat.

Before my parents put plumbing in the house, my brother and I had to take milk cans and assorted containers on a toboggan over the hill to the next farm to get water from a well. We had to prime the pump first with warm water to get the air and water to flow. I would stand next to the abandoned farmhouse near the pump out of the wind to get warmed by the sun. My brother occasionally got upset with me because I wasn't helping. Out of guilt, a sense of responsibility and a desire to get inside our warm house, I would run from my sunny spot and help load the containers on the toboggan. We would pull it up the hill to our house together, complaining all the way. We welcomed the warmth of home, even on sunny winter days.

School was out for the winter holidays so we spent a lot of time tobogganing, sledding, skiing down the hills around our house. We also did a lot of exploring in the woods. Our parents never really knew where we travelled in the forest as long as we made sure we returned home in time for dinner. Behind our house across the hayfield was a deep gulley with a stream. During summer it was the sweetest water anyone could taste.

I remember one particular day when my brother and I found a wounded deer. Overnight 12 inches of snow had fallen which, of course, meant we had to do the shoveling before we could play in the snow. When we were done we took off across the field behind our house towards the stream. Often we would cross over the stone fence bordering our field and the neighboring corn field. Since the sun was shining in a cloudless sky that day we climbed over the wall and made our way to what was once the cellar of a house or barn in the middle of the cow pasture.

We knew we had to be careful because our neighbors set traps to catch rabbits. When we got to the cellar we saw something move. It was a baby deer caught in one of the traps. Carefully and slowly we approached the young deer all the while talking softly hoping to reassure it that we weren't going to hurt it. My brother had an uncanny ability to calm domestic animals on the farms nearby so I let him do what he did best. The damage wasn't too bad since the fawn's leg was too thin to be broken by the trap.

While he calmed the deer I went to work on freeing the injured leg. I took my scarf and wetted it in the snow so I could clean the wound. It took both of us to spring the trap. As soon as we did the baby fawn bolted for the woods. He seemed okay so we went home and I had to explain to Mom why there was blood on my scarf.

A few days later we were again in our neighbor's cow pasture when we saw a doe and two fawns. As we watched them, the doe slowly came over to us and nudged our outstretched hands then she and her fawns disappeared into the protection of the trees. We both felt honored by the doe who had the courage to come close to us to say thank you for helping her baby.

Silently Skeezie crouched into attack posture, eyes focused on her target, a mouse who made the mistake of being in the open field making it an easy catch. While her prey was busy nibbling on some dried wheat seeds she pounced. Unfortunately, the mouse was much faster than Skeezie had anticipated and escaped into the woods. There was nothing else for her to do but shrug and go check on her kittens.

She saw them playing at the tree stump behind the house near the kitchen door. Upon approaching them, there were loud, panicky squeals of discomfort coming from Missy. "They're at it again," she sighed. Sometimes the boys would double team or just attack Missy separately. They didn't mean anything vicious towards one another but were just growing up and learning how to protect themselves. Fortunately Missy was becoming quite good at defending herself as the brothers often gave up and found something else to do.

"Children, you must calm down now. You've annoyed your sister enough," admonished Skeezie.

"Mom, Skudgie and Orangey really hurt me sometimes. Can't you tell them to stop it?" complained Missy.

"It's part of growing up. All of you need to know how to protect yourselves and hunt. Your attempts to catch butterflies and insects or fighting with each other help you to take care of yourselves when you're grown up and on your own," she explained.

"No, Mom, I don't want to leave you," wailed Missy.

"Hush, Little One, just remember you have to be able to take care of yourself first. But gather around me while I tell you about Benji who was an expert hunter," their mother said.

Without hesitation all three stopped what they were doing and obediently lay down in a half circle next to their mother.

Benji Defends His Turf

Benji's person had spent the day digging and planting until finally in late afternoon she was done. Deciding to relax, she made myself comfortable on the deck bench. Benji who was also outside spent most of the day napping and watching his person pretending to be a gardener. Since the late afternoon sun was filtering through the trees Benj joined her on the deck bench which was in the shade. While they sat on the bench a cardinal, wren, gold finch visited the birdfeeder. Benji had no interest in the birds since he had given up trying to catch them because the birdfeeder was too high above the ground..

Eventually Benji woke up from his nap, got up and repositioned himself under the other bench next to the cat tree. His attention became focused on an intruder, the gray squirrel who stubbornly came almost every day to eat some seeds the birds dropped on the ground under the feeder. At the same time each adversary spied the other so it was a case of *"I'm watching you watching me"* for a long, long time. The squirrel tried to hide by flattening its body into the fence top to out-wait Benji. He was indeed a very foolish squirrel! The squirrel really wanted to get the seeds. Several times he made false starts at jumping to the ground but changed his mind. At one point it seemed the trespasser had decided to give up and by way of the fence began going towards his usual exit path. But no, he stopped opposite the feeder, then retraced his steps back to his point of entry into the backyard next to the tree on the other side of the fence. So the staring contest continued.

Meanwhile a red squirrel came jumping from limb to limb on his way to the very same birdfeeder. The interloper reached the neighbor's tree trunk and promptly worked his way to the fence. Upon reaching the fence he noticed the gray squirrel and bid a hasty retreat to the neighbor's yard. And the staring contest continued. After awhile the red squirrel reappeared on the fence. This time he had decided to be bold and held his ground. The gray squirrel started chattering obviously telling the gatecrasher to vacate the premises as he was there first, but no deal. So they both chittered and chattered at each other until the red squirrel climbed up into the tree branches where he was out of sight. But determination took hold of the red squirrel who also wanted his portion of the bounty so he returned to the fence.

Finally the gray squirrel couldn't resist the offering of food. He began to climb down the fence but being so fat he simply fell down with a plop! Instantaneously Benji made his move. He became a streak of black and white fur flying towards the squirrel. Needless to say he scared both squirrels who scuttled up the tree to a safe distance from the predator. They both turned to Benji and gave him a piece of their minds while flipping their tails at him as if they were beating a drum. Wisely both decided that it would be better to retreat and come back another day. The red squirrel climbed to the higher tree limbs retreating quickly by jumping from one tree branch to another. The gray squirrel also climbed after the red squirrel following the same waving tree branches to safety.

Just to make sure they had gone, Benji waited for a long time by the fence for either offender who may have dared to reconvene the battle. Finally deciding they had gotten the point, he stealthily hid himself under the dwarf lilac bush at the fence corner to wait patiently for the next uninvited guest!

It had been a long day. The kittens spent the morning exploring the fields, barn and yard around the house. They tested their hunting skills attempting to catch whatever moved whether a mouse or butterfly, stalking and attacking each other, racing and hopping through the tall grass of the field behind the house, and playing hide-and-seek in the bushes that lined the field. After a most tasty lunch of cow's milk, a mouse and Cook Martha's meat droppings on the kitchen floor, they were ready for a long nap. Their mother Skeezie knew they were tired and decided it was time they got a little rest. She could use some alone time also. There was a cat from the neighboring farm napping in the shade of the Lilac bush. She particularly enjoyed the company of an adult cat just to talk about the local goings-on.

"Okay, Kittens, you've had a very busy day so far. It's time for you to get some rest. I noticed you really had fun exploring around the house and barn today and practicing hunting," said Skeezie corralling her children.

"Mom, that's a great idea, I love your stories!" exclaimed Skudgie.

"Yeah, Mom, I almost caught a mouse but it was too quick for me to grab, do you think we are getting better at hunting?" asked Orangey excitedly.

"All of you are definitely improving but you have a long way to go before you will be able to take care of yourselves. But for now, let's go into the kitchen and settle in our box so we all can get some rest," responded their mother while guiding them to the kitchen door.

Cook Martha had left a bowl of roasted chicken near their box after lunch for the feline family. As soon as the kittens saw the food, they charged all at once to the bowl, gobbled down the food, and as their mother had taught them, delicately cleaned their faces and paws. Without a word from *their mother, all three climbed into the box. Pleased to see they were in bed, Skeezie also got into the cat box and arranged herself around the kittens.*

"Is everyone ready for the story?" she asked smiling because she knew their answer.

"Yes, Mom, we are," meowed all the kittens at once.

Let's Go Exploring

It was snowing all day making the chore of shoveling out the driveway discouraging. The snow would stop, Person would shovel. The snow started again. Person would shovel again. It was a battle Person was destined to lose. Finally, Person put the shovel away and came into the house to ease her aching muscles and warm up. As soon as the door opened she was greeted with two rather loud and annoyed sounding voices.

"Meow!"

Nala, an orange American Tabby, and Benji, a black and white Tuxedo cat greeted her with demanding meows.

"Hey, give me a chance to get inside, cats!" exclaimed Person.

Both cats sat down and waited patiently allowing her to remove her boots and coat,

"Wow, it's really cold out there! Do you cats want to go outside?" she said opening the door.

In response neither of the felines moved, then slowly Nala strolled to the door and stopped next to it. Benji, the more adventurous of the cats, decided he would take the opportunity to go outside. Person held the door open wide so they could see the snow-covered ground and feel the chilly air. Benji ventured onto the porch, inspected it thoroughly and then obviously satisfied with his conclusion jumped atop the railing. Oblivious of the cold snow accumulating on the railing, Benji tucked his paws underneath his body to watch the goings-on in the neighborhood.

"Are you going out, too?" Person inquired of Nala still holding open the door.

Nala just starred at her as if to say "Do you really expect an answer?". Without hesitation she slowly ventured onto the porch.

Benji was the first to retreat from the cold. He gingerly shook his hind legs and jumped onto the porch floor and came inside. So that he didn't seem wimpy, Benji nonchalantly meandered into the kitchen to munch on the food in his dish. Meanwhile Nala made herself comfortable on top of the porch rail and focused on sampling the scents on the chilly air. She appreciated the advantage of a warm winter coat! Shortly thereafter she, too, followed Benji into the kitchen.

Just recently Person and the cats had relocated from the city into a country house. Living in a house was quite a change from their city apartment. As indoor cats they were able to only observe the outside from a fourth floor windowsill. The apartment was in the back with a view into the neighboring buildings. The only interesting activity was watching the pigeons constantly landing on the fire escape or on top of nearby buildings. On the other hand, their country house provided a wide range of outdoor action for enjoyment. People walked by, cars traveled on the street, birds flew from tree to tree, the sun shone in each room and a warm summer breeze flowed from the kitchen window to the living room. The house had two floors and several rooms unlike the three room city apartment. There was plenty of room for everyone, furry cats and humans, to find solitude whenever needed. The felines had devised a competitive game of racing up and down the stairs, through the living room, dining room and kitchen.

Finally the snow and ice melted. The freezing temperatures gradually warmed up giving way to spring which transformed the ground into a flowering wonderland. Summer quickly followed spring bringing warm breezes and pleasant days. Nala and Benji loved lying in the warm sun streaming through the open living room windows.

"Ah, what a wonderful summer day, don't you think, Benji!" exclaimed Nala. Benji lazily opened his eyes from his nap and gazed at Nala dreamily and agreed. "Well, what are we going to do today? You know our Person won't let us outside by ourselves...something about getting lost and not being able to find our way back home," reminded Nala.

"Well, we'll just have to fool her," stated Beni emphatically, "when she goes out the back door we'll just casually follow behind and go to our usual places. She won't pay attention especially since she'll be working in the yard. We can sneak through the space in the fence around the side of the house out of her sight. She most likely thinks we can't get out that way so she won't be checking on us. What do you say, are you up for an adventure?"

"I guess so. Look, she's going outside now. Let's go!" exclaimed Nala before changing her mind.

Without hesitation the cats scooted out the door, down the steps and around the house corner. They found the opening, pushed their heads into the hole and squeezed the rest of their bodies through as if they were experienced burglars. Within a few seconds they were in front of the house on high alert and ready for their adventure. They quickly turned left and trotted down the sidewalk towards the street corner. It was the very same corner they saw from the upstairs bedroom window.

"Do you know where we're going?" asked Nala nervously. "We should be careful since we haven't been in the front of the house by ourselves, you know."

"Oh, stop worrying, just follow me," said Benji with irritation in his voice. "Look, there are some trees ahead, we can hide there."

Without hesitation the cats trotted past some houses across a large open space with gravelly black dirt and reached the trees. They looked furtively around them, then crawled under the bushes near the big trees and lay down.

"Now what?" asked Nala.

"Look, there are some cats over there. Let's ask them where to get food and find a warm place to stay," suggested Benji.

Benji and Nala cautiously sauntered over to the cats sitting on a bench next to a building with a blue roof. They noticed that there were dishes with food crumbs and decided to help themselves. Suddenly a cat on the bench jumped down and expressed his displeasure rather rudely.

"Hey, what are you doing? That's not for you. Get your own food!" he snarled.

Startled, Nala and Benji stopped in their tracks and mid-chew. Neither of them had noticed there was someone watching them from the bench. Benji sized up the intruder very quickly. He was large with long matted fur of black tiger stripes, a white chest and white front paws. His fur was dirty and knotted and in need of grooming. There was a long scar on his nose and his eyes looked at him with a hard, cold stare. His back was arched with claws showing beneath his toes. The striped tabby gave a low warning growl as he prepared to pounce on the strangers. The other cats, a gray tiger, a long-haired black cat and a short-haired gray cat, jumped down from the bench and stood behind their leader making a low growl and showing their sharp nails. Benji immediately realized that he and Nala were in imminent danger and lowered his whole body onto the ground in a submissive crouch.

"We didn't know. We're new to the neighborhood and were just hungry," explained Benji. Cautiously, maintaining his crouch, backing away from the ruffians as he nudged Nala, "We'll be on our way."

They slowly retreated while keeping their eyes on the unsavory pack. As soon as they were at the corner of the blue and white building Nala and Benji quickly picked up the pace scuttling around the building corner. Benji suddenly stopped. There was a white house with a small porch and some bushes by the windows. A short gray fence was next to the shrubs and garbage cans along the driveway side of the house. His first thought was that it was their house. Nala had the same impression as she stared at the house.

"Benji, it's our house!" exclaimed Nala.

"No, it's not. It's too small and has bushes. Besides our porch is painted white and brown. There's a little tree our

Person and Little Person Ambrosia planted at the corner of the house. This isn't it," he said with deep disappointment in his voice. "Let's keep going."

They slid under the bushes sticking close to the house wall. As they neared the edge of the house, they slowed their pace. Benji carefully peered from under the bushes towards the backyard. There were all kinds of cans and pieces of paper scattered on the grass. It didn't look too safe but the larger cans provided hiding places if needed. Noting all the details, Benji quickly scanned the yard's perimeter noticing a hole in a corner that seemed to be well-used.

"Nala, look, over there! It's a path that seems to be used a lot. It must lead to a safe place. Let's take a look."

Nala was hesitant as she was still shaken by their experience with the cat bully. But, knowing they couldn't go back, she slowly nodded her head in agreement. Benji took the lead and ran straight past the side of the house and leaped towards the hole in the fence. Nala was right on his heels in an instant. Both cats dived into the hole and followed the path. Without warning they found themselves facing a large white cement building with huge windows and walls.

"What is this?!" asked Benji in shock. "Wait, this looks like a building I see from the kitchen window. Hey, Nala we must be near home!"

"I have no idea what building you are talking about but I'm tired, hungry and scared. I want to go home."

"I want to go home, too. Being on the street isn't as great as I thought it would be. Those cats were really mean. Come on, we have no place to go but around this building."

The two cats stayed as close to the building wall as possible. As they neared the building corner Benji saw moving boxes with wheels and people passing by. He peeked around the corner and saw more large windows and walls, a wide black dirt space and lots more moving boxes with wheels. His first instinct was to turn back the way they had come but decided to keep going forward. On the right was a really wide paved road with fast moving boxes. Straight ahead was grass, trees and low growing bushes. On the left was a long, wide stone path that led to a door that magically opened every time a human went in or out. Benji knew that Nala depended upon him to lead them to safety and home.

"Let's head for those trees. We should be safe there. Run across that wide road. I think it's for those moving boxes," said Benji.

"I'm frightened. What if one of those moving things hits us? Aren't they dangerous?" asked Nala worriedly.

"Remember, we watch them from the upstairs window. They always go in a straight line so we will have to make sure there isn't one coming and run across as fast as we can."

"Okay," said Nala, "I'm right behind you."

Keeping their eyes on their goal, the cats ran as fast as they could across the street to the safety of the trees. By this time they were totally exhausted as each lay down breathing heavily.

"Let's rest for awhile," said Nala. "We can watch from here without anyone seeing us."

To the cats it seemed like forever since they left the safety of their house. They were very hungry but there didn't seem to be any food nearby. They didn't know how to catch a mouse let alone eat it.

"Look, there are more trees over there and houses," exclaimed Nala. "Do you think we should go over there?"

"We might just as well since there is no other place to go," agreed Benji.

Stealthily the fugitives crept towards the trees. They stopped short at the pavement.

"Oh, no," said Benji in frustration, "there's another wide space! Those things that move so fast on wheels come here, too. Quick, I don't see anything coming, let's run across it to those bushes," he instructed.

"But, which way should we go?" asked Nala nervously.

"I'm not too sure but I have a feeling that we should stay under the trees. If we go the other way there are only buildings and another wide black space. There doesn't seem to be much in the way of protective cover over there." said Benji.

Eventually the cats got up, grouching close to the ground they slinked slowly under cover of the trees towards the houses. Benji looked across the large paved space with the moving wheels things that seemed stuck in the black dirt and noticed a grouping of tall leafy trees. The trees seemed to encircle multi-colored wooden houses. There were fences. Dogs barked. Benji halted. Listened. A memory was gradually coming forward. It was all so familiar. So familiar that he knew they were going in the right direction.

"Nala, see those buildings over there with the fences? I recognize them. They are the ones we see from the back window of Person's kitchen," Benji said with excitement in his voice.

Nala followed his gaze and agreed that they did look familiar.

"We're going to run. See where the trees end? From there we will have to run towards the houses. But be careful, I remember there are dogs living in those houses," Benji said decisively.

As soon as the opportunity presented itself, both cats ran as if their lives depended upon it...which it did. Suddenly they heard dogs barking. Benji knew they were close to home but still not out of danger. He nudged Nala, signaling they had better get going before the dogs started chasing them. She begrudgingly nodded her head and followed him.

"Let's keep going this way. Those dogs may be dangerous," cautioned Benji.

As the cats crossed the yards of each house's backyard keeping close to the fences, they heard a loud, rough threatening voice.

"Hey, what are you doing in my yard. I don't like cats so you better run. Get out of my yard. Now!" growled a large dark brown and black dog who was sitting on a porch. He jumped down from his perch and ran after them barking loudly.

Benji and Nala didn't know what to do. They couldn't run into the next yard because there were two more dogs waiting for them. Benji made an instinctive decision and ran towards the front of the houses. He frantically scanned the houses for a safe place where they could hide. Suddenly he saw a brown house at the corner on one side and a large red colored stone building across from the narrow paved path that ran in front of the houses. His heart soared. He felt they were really close to their Person's house! He guided Nala up to the corner and ran under a bush growing next to the brown house. Nala quickly followed, her eyes wide with fear and apprehension. Then Benji saw it!

"Nala, we're home! There's Person's porch! See, we're home!" shouted Benji ecstatically.

The cats joyously ran past the parked moving wheel boxes and practically flew up the steps onto their porch. They were home! Nala sat quietly on the top step while Benji meowed at the door.

"What if Person isn't home?" asked Nala with worry in her voice.

"Then we wait," said Benji matter of factly.

Suddenly the front door opened and there was Person! They were so happy to see her that they just meowed and meowed rubbing against her legs.

"What are you two doing out here?" asked Person in surprise. "I thought you were inside. Come on in before you get lost," she said opening the door to let them inside.

Person gave them some food and afterwards both felines were content and happy.

"You know what, Benji," said Nala, "from now on I will stay in the backyard and on the porch. No more wanting to see the world. There are too many mean humans and creatures out there. I'll just watch from the windows in safety."

"Well, I still want to explore but not for a long time. It's good to be home!" said Benji contentedly.

ABOUT THE AUTHOR

Carol Lumm was born and raised in Upstate New York. Upon graduation from high school she relocated to New York City for several years where she earned a Masters of Arts in Linguistics & Literacy and a Master's of Science in Education specializing in TESOL from The City College of New York. She also was employed for several years in advertising for a farm magazine and in adult education for a healthcare union. She returned to Upstate New York and is currently enjoying the pursuit of many interests as a retiree. In addition to her son, she has 5 grandchildren.

Her interest in writing was developed in Junior High School long before the development of computerized technology. She was a prolific writer and researcher in completing assigned research papers often handwriting 20+ pages. Also, Carol engaged in the art of letter writing by penning letters full of news and thoughts of 4 pages or more to friends and relatives. She became interested in writing novels and plays while at SUNY at Albany as part of a theater ensemble. This interest expanded over several years culminating in the goal of publishing her writings so others may share in the adventure.

Other poems and stories by Ms. Lumm have been published in *Seasons of Our Lives* (2019) by the Scribblers writing group and *Voices of Three Burgos Women*, a collection of writings by two sisters-in-law and a granddaughter (2020).

Made in the USA
Middletown, DE
28 July 2024

58057840R00103